The Witchling Apprentice

The Skinwalker Witchling Trilogy

Book 1

B. Kristin McMichael

Lexia Press, LLC
P.O. Box 982
Worthington, OH 43085
www.lexiapress.com

ISBN-10: 1-941745-88-1
ISBN-13: 978-1-941745-88-5

Cover design: Jessica Allain
Editor: Kathie Middlemiss of Kat's Eye Editing
Melissa of There For You Editing
Proofing: Ashton M. Brammer

CONTENTS

CHAPTER 1

Tick ... Tick ... Tick ...

Cassandra Booth tried to ignore the clock as it clicked away from above the desk beside her. It was nerve-wracking enough knowing that if you wanted to take the test to be an apprentice witch you had to do it in front of at least fifty people. However, the clock reminding her it was just about to start was driving her nuts.

Tick ... Tick ... Tick ...

Cassie tried to go over each step of the potion she was making in her head. She needed to concentrate and ignore the noises around her as the room began to fill up with high schoolers.

Tick ... Tick ...

The sound was lost in the now-growing sound of students talking. Unfortunately, that wasn't any better. She glanced up at the room in front of her. Mistake. It was almost half-full of people. No one was looking directly at her, but that didn't make it any easier. Cassie was anxious enough sitting in the lecture area alone, on display, but now there were students who would be watching and talking about her.

Cassie kept her eyes locked on the table and all her supplies. Taking inventory was easy. Doing the actual potion and saying the spell correctly was supposed to be the hard part. No one in her high school, let alone grade, was even attempting to make the protection spell that had been assigned to her and which would move her from witchling up to the level of junior apprentice. Most people were shocked when she'd asked. It had been many years since a high school student had apprenticed, but that wasn't going to stop Cassie. She was ready to get out of her boring classes. She was ready to join everyone in obtaining the great knowledge that came with being a full-time member of the coven. Cassie was ready to belong.

Life hadn't always kept Cassie an outsider. When she was younger, she had tons of friends and fit in fine. It changed as she grew, and it was even more evident now as she sat in front of the room. There was only one person smiling excitedly and encouraging her with what she was about to do. Just one person.

Cassie smiled meekly at the stunning blonde in the front row. Whitney smiled back with her movie-star smile.

'You can do it,' she mouthed to Cassie, putting two thumbs up. At least she had the confidence Cassie was slowly losing.

Whitney was exactly the opposite of Cassie. She was tall, blonde, willowy, and a magnet for every guy in school. Cassie was a stark contrast with her dark bob-cut brown hair, height just over five feet tall with her shoes on, and not a single date in all of her life. Whitney seemed to thrive on the attention, but not all the time. Whitney was human after all, and did like a moment alone. That was how Cassie first met her.

The door around the back of the last math room where the junior and senior high schools connected could be propped open, and no one would notice. Cassie often snuck outside to sit alone when the day got too hectic, and only two weeks into their eighth-grade year Whitney also found the wonderfully quiet spot. They'd been going there together ever since.

She looked back down at her supplies. It was overwhelming to stand in front of everyone. She had prepared for the test, practiced making the potion, and said the spell over a hundred times. Cassie had figured out the secret ingredient that would make it all work, but she hadn't counted on how it would feel to be on display, and the exam hadn't even started. It was bad with everyone lounging around, talking to their friends. It would only be worse once they were all focused on her.

Closing her eyes, she took a deep breath. Opening them to look at the latest group of students that entered, she groaned to herself. Why in the world were the jocks coming to her test? Atwood High was combined with students that were studying witchcraft and would join the local coven, and students that knew about magic but didn't practice it. The jocks were part of the group that didn't practice. Cassie wanted to object to the teacher that just entered, but the room went quiet at Mrs. Anton's entry. It was too late to kick the jocks out.

Cassie hid her scowl as she looked up at the top of the room. Her only other friend, Owen Malla, was sitting in the middle of the group of football players in the back row. Owen grinned at her and gave her a thumbs-up also. Next to him sat the school heartthrobs, Nathaniel Bay and Abe Jones, listening to their fourth friend Nic Teller talk about something. Owen went back to their conversation, laughing at whatever joke was told, even though the room was almost completely quiet otherwise. Cassie's short burst of confidence from his thumbs-up quickly disappeared.

Mrs. Anton stood up and addressed the class. Cassie didn't listen as her stomach turned in circles. It wasn't butterflies, but more like a whirl of birds, like those ones from the latest horror movie Cassie had been watching the night before. They were going to peck their way out if she had to sit much longer.

Mrs. Anton smiled and stepped back, nodding to Cassie.

She took a deep breath.

Cassie tried to give herself a pep talk. *You can do this*. A deep breath was all she needed.

One last glance to the room wasn't helpful in the least.

Whoever thought it was a good idea to picture everyone in the room naked had never been in a room like this. The four hottest guys in the school were in the top row, and Whitney was in the front. Cassie didn't want to picture any of them naked!

With shaky hands, Cassie reached for the first vial. Luckily, the test was to make the potion, but not to tell anyone how she did it. The 'how' was completely up to her. Cassie grasped the vial and began to uncork the liquid. Mixing it first was the key to doing the potion right or wrong. She began to concentrate on the vial in her hand and the room around her dimmed out.

Time passed quickly as she mixed liquids and herbs together. One after another she followed the steps she had internalized. Pulverize the plants into the right form of paste. Mix with another solution. Carefully put the first liquid with the second. Mix gently. Prepare the next plant. Mix and keep going. Repeat and keep going. One by one, each ingredient was added to the mixture. She didn't pay attention to the room as she heated the water up. That had to be added second to last. The water heated and began to steam. Cassie removed it from the archaic Bunsen burner that she had borrowed from the chem lab. She slowly counted to ten to assure herself that it wasn't too hot before adding it to the paste she had already made. Slowly, she mixed it together. It was almost done.

The last ingredient was actually the most important, but she had to be discreet. The instructions to pass the test were to make the potion with only what was present at the table. Cassie could bring any herb she wanted, but everything she was using had been thoroughly searched before she began to make sure no one else had prepared the potion for her. Cassie slipped her hand down to the knife that she had left sitting out behind the coffee-mug-sized bowl she was mixing in. Sucking in her breath, she bit down on her lip as she sliced her finger on the knife, out of view of the classroom before her. It hurt as much as she had expected it would during practice, but at least at home she could curse herself for not having a better way to add her blood. Now she couldn't let the pain show on her face. It wasn't that Cassie thought she was breaking the rules—she *was* using just what was at the table—but she didn't want to let anyone know, just in case.

Cassie stuck her bleeding finger into the mix of herbs and heard a few people chuckle as she did so. She scrunched the warm water into the paste with her bleeding finger. She felt the sting and again had to bite her tongue to keep from giving the secret away. Cassie continued to mush the paste into a thinner liquid until the pain from the cut dulled. Once she was sure the bleeding had stopped, Cassie pulled her hand out and wiped it on the cloth next to her. Taking the mushed up potion, she poured it over a cheese cloth to take out the chunks. Cassie let out her breath when she saw that the liquid was only lightly tinged orange from her blood. No one would notice the difference. It was much better than her last practice run.

After pouring the liquid into the vial the teacher had waiting for her, she touched a few drops to the plant next to it. The plant instantly flowered, meaning the potion had been prepared correctly. Cassie let out another sigh. It was done. Mrs. Anton didn't approach as Cassie finished; she sat in her chair and just stared at her.

First, Cassie glanced at Whitney, and then around the room. Not a single person was speaking, but all sat staring at her. She looked quickly at the plant again. Had she done something wrong? The single rose had opened, as had several more around it. That wasn't exactly what was supposed to happen, but it couldn't be bad. She was to make the protection potion. When finished correctly, it would cause the rosebud to open. What difference did it make if it opened a few extra? She'd done it. The potion was made. She had passed her exam.

She looked to Mrs. Anton, who now had her phone out and was walking out of the room.

Cassie wanted to ask if she passed, but Mrs. Anton was outside the door before Cassie could get a word out.

She looked back to the room to discover everyone still had their eyes trained on her. It was bad before the test, but now all fifty eyes were staring at her like she had grown a second head. Cassie quickly found Whitney's gaze, and even she was gawking. Whitney quickly whipped her hanging mouth into a smile to reassure her, but Cassie had seen it. Why was everyone shocked?

The bell rang, and Cassie realized that she had spent the entire class making the potion. Students were all roused from their staring and began to stand to leave the room. A few continued to peek back at her as they left. Cassie caught Owen grinning as he followed his friends. He snuck a look back at her and gave her another thumbs-up. At least he didn't look shocked by all of it.

The room emptied, and Cassie wasn't sure what to do. Her potion was done, but the teacher had left. Was that how it was supposed to be? By opening more than one flower, maybe that meant she did it wrong. Whitney hurried over to Cassie.

"Did I pass?" Cassie asked her. She hoped her best friend knew more than she did because Cassie was now completely confused. For some reason, she'd had the idea that everyone would clap, and Mrs. Anton would congratulate her on her potion.

"Pass?" Whitney asked in reply, shocked at Cassie's words.

"Miss Booth," Mrs. Anton said as she came back into the room, "I would like to hold onto that for you. Your induction will be in two weeks, and we wouldn't want to lose the proof that you did this before then. I'll keep it locked in my room for you."

Mrs. Anton didn't wait for an answer but took the vial

that held Cassie's potion and briskly walked out of the room.

"Induction?" Cassie was shocked. "I passed." It was a statement but still sounded like a question.

"If we were playing baseball, you didn't just hit the ball, you'd have hit a homerun," Whitney added, throwing her arm around a shocked Cassie's shoulder and ushering her out of the classroom. "That was so awesome."

Cassie was still numb. She had practiced and knew what she was doing, but she hadn't expected that it would actually work and be what they wanted it to be. The stars must have aligned. She had tried her hardest, and it was finally paying off.

"Did you see her face? She wasn't expecting that at all from you," Whitney continued to talk.

Cassie let out a nervous giggle. She really had nothing to be nervous about, but she was still wondering about Mrs. Anton's reaction. Cassie was used to sometimes seeing her classmates in awe when she could do something they didn't expect, but she wasn't used to a teacher just walking away. It had to mean something.

"How long did you have to practice?" Whitney asked, pulling Cassie with her down the crowded hallway.

Whitney was nowhere near doing any sort of witch exam. She didn't put any time into studying, and really didn't seem to care if she were stuck at witchling status forever. Cassie cared because she wanted freedom from her life, which was currently controlled by her uncle. He was far too restrictive. This was her way out.

Once they made it official, Cassie wouldn't have to attend afternoon classes at school and instead would get to choose a mentor to work under in the community. For three hours a day, Cassie would be out from under her uncle's smothering control. There was an alternative to the test, but she refused to listen to Whitney's logic. Uncle John wouldn't get a say in anything Cassie did when she turned eighteen, but that was too far away. Two years were too long to wait.

Whitney threaded her arm through Cassie's and pulled her down the hallway when Cassie didn't answer. It didn't matter to Whitney; she was used to it with her best friend.

"Don't look now, but I think the entire football team is impressed with you," Whitney whispered as they walked by a group of guys.

Cassie snuck a glance anyway. Wasn't the phrase 'don't look now' code for 'sneak a look'?

Owen was beaming at her when she passed. She expected that. He was excited for her before she took the test. It was actually at his suggestion that she decided to take it early. Most of the students took it at the end of their senior year, but he figured she could do it now.

As Cassie returned her gaze to the floor while Whitney pulled her along, she caught the eye of the player next to Owen. Owen's best friend and football receiver extraordinaire was staring at her. His crystal-clear blue eyes sparkled and a sly grin formed on his lips when he noticed her looking.

Cassie couldn't help the redness that burned in her cheeks. She'd had a crush on Nate for forever—even before he changed his nickname to Than, which he did because it sounded cooler and made him fit into the cool crowd.

Whitney bumped Cassie's shoulder.

"Don't look now, but I think Than is looking at you," she whispered to Cassie.

Cassie didn't need to check it out again. She had already seen, and she hated that her heart was beating faster. It didn't make a difference if he saw her now or not. He was completely out of her league. Nate was one of the popular people, and Cassie was far from it. It didn't matter to her anyway, as she had Whitney and Owen as real friends. Besides, her uncle would never allow her to do something as normal as dating, even if she had finally caught Nate's eye. Life didn't work that way for Cassie.

As long as she remembered, Cassie had felt like an outsider to the town. Passing her exam was the first step to being included in everything, whether Uncle John wanted her to be included or not. She was ready to join the world around her.

Cassie slowly walked through the empty halls of Atwood High. Good thing Saturdays were always quiet. Looking around, she found that there was just something different about the hallways when they weren't filled with students. She kind of preferred it that way. Cassie passed her own locker and didn't stop to read the note that was still sticking out of the air vent at the top. It had to be from Whitney. And Cassie didn't want to have to explain to her the fact that she had basically gone over her uncle's head to do the exam the day before. She had hinted that she wasn't planning to tell Uncle John, but Whitney still thought she had to get permission. Whitney, while a great friend, still just didn't understand what Cassie's life was like at all.

Reaching for the door handle to the labs, she paused as someone came from around the corner. She quickly went into the room and shut the door behind her. The lights were still off in the room, and Cassie didn't try to turn them on. She wasn't in the mood to deal with anyone.

The people in the hallway walked closer, and Cassie wished she could hide behind her lab bench in case she needed to cast an invisibility spell to avoid whoever it was.

Cassie held her breath as the people stopped not too far away.

"Do you think she'll be at the dance?" one asked the other.

"I hope so. My mother told me that she's probably the most powerful witch of our generation," the other voice replied. They were both guys, but Cassie had no clue who they were.

"My parents said the same thing," the first replied.

Cassie's heart beat faster, and she tried her best to not move or make a single sound. They were discussing who the adults thought was the most powerful witch. Uncle John never talked about anything like that. Uncle John didn't talk about much of anything. If it wasn't for Aunt Maria, Cassie wouldn't have learned a single thing about her ancestry.

"And you know that it means whomever she chooses to be her mate will get all that power, too."

Mate? Cassie was more confused than ever, even though it was her natural state of being. She always felt like she was missing the punch line to the secret in school and around town, but these guys were just strange.

"Man, I'd give anything to be the one she chooses," the first said as they started to move away.

"Like she'd choose a bird brain like you." The second started to laugh.

Cassie listened as they grew too faint to hear what they were saying. Weird as it may have been, and it was also a bit of a disappointment. Cassie had hoped by taking the exam and passing she would finally be told what she was missing. Whitney was the only one that didn't seem to be keeping things from her. At times, it actually seemed like Whitney knew less about the witches in town than she did. But her passing the day before didn't open any new doors. It was still the same.

The neat, orderly desks had been washed since class on Friday, and everything had a clean lemony smell. She gave the guys a few more seconds before she reached for the classroom light. Cassie was going to miss the lab room the most. Now that she passed she would have no more witch classes at school. She still had to attend the normal morning classes, but her favorite part of the day would be gone. She clicked the light on, and her eyes quickly adjusted to the brightness in the room.

It will be worth it, Cassie repeated in her head. She had

been saying that to herself since she turned in her 'Intention to Test' slip a week ago.

Cassie nearly screamed when she noticed someone lying across one of the desks like a cat, curled up to keep warm using body heat. She would know those blonde curls anywhere.

"Gosh, are you trying to give me a heart attack?" Cassie complained to Whitney.

Whitney yawned and stretched her arms above her head. Slowly and more gracefully than Cassie could ever imagine being, Whitney stood.

"Guess you didn't stop by your locker. If you had, you wouldn't have gotten scared."

She had Cassie there.

"I went to your place, and John said you were here. I had no clue you were coming to school today," she continued.

Not completely awake yet, Whitney stood and leaned against the nearest desk.

"Just stopping by to clean out my lab bench since I don't have class anymore," Cassie replied.

"Figured that much. I'd join you if they'd let me," Whitney complained. She hated the witch classes with a passion.

Cassie made her way back to the last bench in the back of the room. Opening the drawers, she began to take the jars out one at a time. As she placed them on a tray, Whitney was finally awake enough from her nap to join her.

"Can't I have that one?" Whitney asked, pointing to the vial from class the day before.

"Why not?" Cassie replied and handed it over. Cassie didn't have to pass the class anymore, and it wasn't like it was cheating. Everyone already knew Whitney wasn't going to ace the class. No one would actually believe she made it anyway, but if she wanted to try to pass it off as her own, Cassie wasn't about to stop her.

"Have you thought any more about who you want to

apprentice with?" Whitney asked as she continued to look through Cassie's vials with her.

"No. I want to talk with Aunt Maria, but she's still on retreat. I think they're punishing her," Cassie added, leaving out the exact reason why.

Aunt Maria had warned Cassie she would be punished before they had gone into the backward sidhe witch village, but she didn't want to say no to Devin. He'd been a friend for several years, and she said that she owed him. Cassie was more than happy to break the rules and not tell anyone, but it seemed that it didn't matter. The coven knew where they had been the whole time. Once they returned, Maria had been sent on assignment after assignment. Cassie kind of felt bad. Her aunt was the only witch in town that Cassie really knew, and without her around she felt a bit lonely.

"Too bad they don't let you apprentice with family," Whitney added what Cassie had already thought.

Family would have been the perfect solution if it were possible. Cassie didn't know why, but she always felt like she wasn't part of the group with the witches. They let her learn, and she took all the classes, but it just seemed off. It could have been because everyone was afraid to look her in the eyes—everyone knew she had the ability to see a person's soul inside their eyes—but it seemed like more than just that. Others in town could do even weirder stuff than that, and they didn't seem like outcasts.

"Is that all?" Whitney asked, looking into the empty drawer.

Cassie glanced down at everything that was left over and took the supplies she would use. The rest wasn't her problem. The teachers would probably put it all back in stock. Cassie wasn't one for using everything they gave her like other students.

"Yep," Cassie replied, shutting the drawer.

"Good. That gives us plenty of time to get ready for the dance." Whitney placed her hand over Cassie's mouth before she could protest. "Mrs. Sherman already gave me permission to use the girl's locker room to change and get ready in."

Cassie glared at her friend and down at the hand still covering her mouth.

"Before you complain, I already bought you a dress and shoes, and your uncle said *yes* to you going." Whitney dropped her hand.

Cassie was at a loss for words. Uncle John never allowed her to go out, let alone to a dance, even if she had wanted to. It had to be a joke.

"We don't have enough time to go out to eat, but I brought burgers from Jimmies." Whitney pushed Cassie toward the door.

"But," Cassie finally sputtered.

"But, but, but." Whitney *tsk*ed her. "I told John that I was taking you to the dance. Not some guy. Just a 'girls at the dance' thing. I called my mother to deal with him. After ten minutes of her on the phone, he easily agreed."

Whitney's mother was not only a leader in the coven but also a lawyer, a really good lawyer. No one stood a chance arguing with her.

"She didn't tell him about the test?" Cassie quickly realized that it wasn't a good idea to have others from the coven talking to her uncle quite yet, at least until she found a way to tell him.

"No. Because I didn't tell her," Whitney added, grabbing Cassie's bag which she had dropped at the doorway earlier.

Cassie raised her eyebrows as Whitney continued to pull her down the hallway toward the gym. Atwood was a small town. It was very rare that someone didn't know everything that was going on. Cassie was holding her breath all week to her uncle finding out beforehand, and since he didn't, she kind of felt like she got off scot-free ... that was at least until she really did have to tell him. Then he was going to be ticked off. Cassie hoped that her birthday would shock him into reality in a couple months when she turned seventeen, but she kind of had hoped he would stay oblivious to her new status until she was eighteen.

"Really. She didn't say a thing. I was beside her the whole time. She just argued that you had to get out of the house, and a chaperoned school dance was safer than a date with a boy." Whitney shrugged. "You know, the whole 'these girls are growing up' and the 'we have to let the birds leave the nest some time' speeches."

Cassie could smell the burgers as Whitney pulled her into the locker room. On their favorite bench, two places were set up with burgers, fries, and milkshakes waiting to be eaten. Cassie's stomach growled in response to the meal before them.

"See? I'm a great date. Best friends are so much better than boyfriends. I knew you'd be hungry, and had food waiting. Dinner and dancing. Isn't that a great first date? I know you'd like it better if I were Than," Whitney teased, sitting down on her side of the bench, and grabbing her burger.

"Not in a thousand years. I'm completely over him," Cassie replied.

"Sure, sure," Whitney responded with a mouthful of food. "Like one can just get over Nathaniel Bay."

Cassie sat down and started to eat as well. It didn't matter how many times she told Whitney she wasn't interested in Nate anymore, Whitney always brought him up. Cassie was ready to move on with a new crush; she just had to find one first.

"So how's it feel?" Whitney asked between bites. She was obviously as hungry as Cassie.

"How does what feel?" Cassie asked. The burgers tasted like burgers. There was nothing to feel.

"Passing your exam, the protection spell," Whitney replied and rolled her eyes at Cassie.

Cassie shrugged. She didn't feel anything yet. She felt

like the protection spell wasn't complete. She had added the correct ingredients and made it correctly, but she was pretty sure the spell included using it on herself. Why else was the protection spell the one thing she needed to do to pass from witchling to apprentice? She felt nothing after her test yesterday or even today. But last summer? Now that felt real. Her trip to the sidhe witch village included lots of spell and potion practice, and was the most exciting thing she had ever done in her life. Counteracting someone else's spell and breaking a blood bond? That was exciting; challenging, but fun.

"Breaking a blood bond?" Whitney asked in shock.

Cassie covered her mouth. She had said it out loud.

"You have to promise you never heard that." Cassie turned to her best friend. It had been torture to keep her summer adventure from Whitney. "Maria will be in more trouble if anyone knows."

"My mother said Maria took you on an unauthorized trip, but she never mentioned doing magic on the trip," Whitney stated, proving that she partially knew something already.

"No one knows that," Cassie added. That explained Maria's constant workload. They just thought Maria had taken her on a trip.

"Of course not. Maria would be in a lot more trouble by now," Whitney replied, taking another bite of her food, but not removing her eyes from Cassie. "Where'd she take you?"

"To another village of magic users," Cassie replied, unsure how much to tell her. Whitney's mother had a lot of power in the coven, and Cassie didn't want to get either Maria or Whitney in trouble.

Whitney's eyes got larger. "She didn't. You aren't allowed to visit other magic villages until you join the coven." Whitney didn't take another bite. She was just staring at Cassie.

Cassie shrugged. "It's not that big of a deal. The sidhe

were actually nice … well, at least the few we met. We were there to help Devin. Remember that really cute blond that visited years ago?"

"Sidhe?" Whitney sputtered, food coming out of her mouth.

"Yeah, they practice some sort of earthy, Mother Nature magic. Not my kind of stuff," Cassie replied with a shrug. The little magic she saw them do was cool, but their lifestyle of living in the woods in a community made in the trees seemed a little off. Having no modern conveniences at all was a bit much for Cassie's tastes.

"She took you to the sidhe." Whitney's eyes were still bugging out.

Cassie realized that she had just said more than she should have.

"Please don't tell anyone. Maria is already in trouble," Cassie replied, trying to cover up that she now gave an exact location of where they went.

"No one would believe me if I did." Whitney shook her head with a laugh. "The sidhe don't let people visit and leave. Once you enter their village, you stay for life. If I said that's where you went, everyone would call me crazy."

"You've heard of them?" Cassie asked in reply. She had never heard of them, but then again, no one acted strangely around Whitney or withheld information.

"Yeah. My parents have spoken about them before." Whitney finished off her burger and began to eat the fries just as quickly, leaving no room to talk more.

Cassie nodded. She would give anything to have parents around to explain all the weird stuff in the witch world to her. There were many reasons Cassie wished for her mother and father to be with her, and this just added to the list. Cassie had to wonder how much more she could have learned with parents to talk to, or at least to eavesdrop in on. Whitney was great at overhearing the things her mother said.

"Let's do makeup and hair first to keep the dresses

clean." Whitney finally was able to speak again.

Cassie quickly shoved the last of her burger in her mouth. No time for fries. Even if she didn't exactly want to go to the dance, there was no way she wanted to go half done up. Homecoming was almost as formal as prom, or so Cassie had been told. She was in her junior year of high school and had thus far, in thanks to Uncle John, gone to neither of them.

"Hurry up, girlie," Whitney called from the sinks across from the locker benches. "We only have seventy-five minutes to get ready."

Cassie rolled her eyes. Seventy-five minutes would be plenty of time for Whitney. She looked great no matter if she were wearing a little or a lot of makeup. Cassie hoped seventy-five would be enough time for herself, though. She sadly glanced one last time at her fries and shake.

"But my food," Cassie complained, slowly standing.

"We can go out afterward for more," Whitney added as she came back to their locker room cubby. She stood with her hands on her hips just waiting to stop Cassie from delaying the inevitable.

Cassie was trying to hide her hesitation of going to the dance. She didn't particularly love crowds, but she was more worried about the dress in the garment bag next to her.

Whitney hooked her arm in Cassie's to pull her away from the food; she was only using it as an excuse anyways.

"We'd better," Cassie replied. "I'm not a good date when I'm hungry." Whether or not she wanted to go to the dance—which she secretly did but would never tell Whitney—it was time to get ready.

CHAPTER 2

Cassie stood just outside the locker room doors in the shadow they created. She could see the whole elaborately decorated gym, but no one saw her. Her hair was mostly pulled back, and the loose ringlets that fell to frame her face were tempting to curl in her fingers as she nervously watched the crowd. Whitney had already walked into the group of students and was lost in the sea of sparkly dresses. Cassie tugged at the short purple number she was wearing. The dress was more of a shirt on her taller friend, so Whitney assumed it would make a great dress on Cassie. Cassie didn't agree with the assumption, but there was nothing she could do now. The dance was already going, and the short dress was better than nothing. It wasn't like Cassie owned anything as nice, either. Uncle John would be boiling mad by now if he could see her.

From her dark corner, Cassie watched the students dance to the fast beat of the song that was playing. Taking a deep breath, she tried to reassure herself that it was fine. For one night, she would fit in with everyone else. Couples moved in sync while friends laughed and danced in groups. Nope. Cassie wasn't about to fit in, or leave the shadows of her blackened corner spot.

As people laughed and had fun, Cassie knew that this wasn't for her. Dances weren't her thing. Atwood High wasn't her thing. Cassie didn't fit in, and never would. She turned to leave, but the parting crowd caught her attention. Whitney in her all-white, sparkly dress walked through to Cassie's hiding spot like she knew that Cassie was just seconds from bolting.

"I got us a table on the other side of the gym," Whitney yelled over the music as she reached forward and grabbed Cassie's arm. "We can see everything from there. You wouldn't believe how uncoordinated Elijah Miller is. You'd think he's trying to invent a new dance."

Cassie wanted to protest. In fact, running as quick as she could back into the locker room sounded like the best plan. Unfortunately, Whitney turned to her, almost as if she could sense her hesitation. Whitney's eyes locked on her own, and Cassie could sense the feeling coming. It wasn't like she only could tell if a person was good or bad, but often times, and especially with Whitney, Cassie could almost hear the thoughts that were directed at her. Whitney was begging Cassie to join her. The dance meant so much to her. No one ever asked Whitney to the dances, even though she was one of the most beautiful people in the school. She was just as much of an outcast as Cassie was. This was Whitney's one dance. She had begged her mother for over a week to get John to let Cassie come, as if there was no way she was going on her own. Whitney needed Cassie to stay and join her. She wanted to be there with her best friend.

Cassie broke her gaze with Whitney and reluctantly let her lead them through the mass of bodies. The music pounded, and people around her moved to the beat. Whitney led the way to the other side of the gym, which had more than a dozen round tables set up. The one in the back was empty of people, but it had two piles of desserts and drinks at it.

"Figured you'd forgive me with chocolate," Whitney told Cassie, not having to shout as they were the farthest from the speakers in the room.

"I suppose," Cassie replied, reaching for the chocolate bar that was the closest to her.

Whitney had been right. Cassie hadn't noticed, but the tables were set up on a platform to the side of the gym. In her concentration to avoid dancing people, Cassie must have stepped up at some point. The raised tables gave them a great vantage point to watch everything. Not many people joined them at the tables with food, and almost every person in the gym was partnered up with someone. No one seemed to notice Cassie and Whitney as they sat and giggled.

The music changed to a slower song. It was a bit more peaceful than the thumping beat of the one that had just ended. Cassie took another bite of the chocolatey goodness that was on her plate and tried not to sigh. Chocolate was a bit of a weakness of hers.

"Forgive me now?" Whitney asked, genuinely concerned.

Cassie was unsure if she was joking or not. Whitney had intended for her to see everything when she looked into her eyes before, but she was unsure how she was supposed to react. She seemed really worried about Cassie running off.

Reaching over, she gave her friend a half hug.

"Forgive you for what?" Cassie asked innocently like she hadn't just been about to bolt and leave Whitney alone at the dance.

"Good. Now will you still forgive me after this song ends?" Whitney asked, glancing around.

Cassie scrunched up her face. *What in the world is Whitney talking about?* A shadow loomed over Cassie, and she looked up to find a guy she had seen before but didn't even know the name of standing before her.

"Wanna dance?" he asked, his voice cracking.

She looked to Whitney, assuming she knew who the guy was and that he was there for her. Whitney was the one with perfect blonde hair and blue eyes to match. The one with the toothpaste-commercial-perfect smile. Whitney shook her head discreetly as if she knew exactly what Cassie was thinking.

"Me?" Cassie asked as she turned to the guy who was nervously waiting. All five-foot-nothing of her compared to Whitney seemed like it had to be a joke.

"Yes. You, Cassie. Do you want to dance?" he asked with more confidence.

"Um, sure," Cassie replied, unsure what to do exactly.

It wasn't like she was against dancing, but she didn't know the guy asking. Cassie tried to catch Whitney's eye again, but she was looking all over the gym.

Cassie stood up and followed the tall guy to the edge of the dance floor, not too far away from Whitney. Cassie slowed down as the guy began to walk into the middle of the swaying bodies. She wasn't too sure she wanted to be that close to everyone. She had gotten better over the years at not looking too closely into people's eyes and seeing what she really didn't want to see, but it still accidentally happened every now and then. The relaxed people in the group were prime targets for it to happen; not exactly what Cassie wanted to be doing.

The guy who had asked her to dance glanced back over his shoulder at Cassie like he sensed she had stopped moving. As his gaze stopped behind her, he halted in his tracks and turned back to Cassie, reaching for her waist to pull her closer to dance.

"She's a bit protective of you, isn't she?" he commented as he leaned down to talk to Cassie. He had at least ten inches of height on her.

Cassie looked back over her shoulder at her friend. Whitney smiled and gave a little finger wave to the both of them.

"I suppose," Cassie replied, unsure what the guy was talking about. Whitney was just watching.

"I'm Kevin, by the way," the guy finally introduced himself. "I think you have English next door to my class for first period."

Cassie craned her neck back to look up at him. It was awkward to dance with someone that much taller than her, but even more awkward to have a conversation with someone she didn't know yet who seemed to know her. Her first and only dance was ranking up on the weird scale that was her life lately.

"I'm in Mrs. Merrill's class," Cassie replied.

She didn't recognize him at all. She had a feeling he was a senior. She knew almost everyone in her own class of juniors, and a few in the freshman class since Whitney had a little brother, but she didn't know any students in the other grades. Girls were hard enough to keep track of, but since her afternoons were spent in witchling classes that were all female, she really didn't know any of the guys in the other grades. She just smiled and shrugged. That had to work.

Cassie felt a tap on her shoulder, and she turned to look at the person interrupting their dance. Another boy she didn't recognize was standing there, waiting for her to look at him. She caught his eyes briefly and didn't need to delve further to know that he wanted to dance with her also. Her tall, older dancing partner glared at the intruder.

"I was hoping I could get a dance in also," he said as the music was slowly ending, his timing perfect to cut her current dance short.

Cassie's first dancer didn't like that they were being interrupted, but she didn't plan to stick around for a second dance anyway. A new song started in a fast tempo, and Cassie took that as her cue to ditch both the guys.

"I need to go back to Whitney," she told the two guys. "Maybe the next slow one." She didn't care which one interpreted that as a yes, but she sure wasn't interested in dancing with either. It was way too strange.

Whitney grinned at Cassie as she sat back down.

"So that wasn't too bad now, was it?" Whitney asked. "Kevin is pretty cute."

"Really?" Cassie replied with a rolling of her eyes.

"Oh yeah, I forgot. You still have a crush on Than," Whitney replied. Whitney never knew Nate as Nate, but had heard enough from Owen to know that Cassie had had a crush on Nate for years.

"No. I'm not interested in anyone. I think I'll need to find a boyfriend not from around here. Too many people here know me and what I can do. I never get a straight answer, or can get anyone to look me in the eyes for that matter," Cassie complained. She had already decided that years ago. The guys in town were not for her.

Very few people knew that Cassie had control of her extra powers now. Most of the people remembered her as a child that would accidentally "see" too much. It was creepy when she would answer questions she wasn't asked, and worse when she would accidentally see a secret. After a couple times of speaking what she saw, Cassie knew she had screwed up. But that didn't matter. She had already been labeled as an outcast.

"Don't worry. You'll always have Owen. It's not like he's going anywhere, and I heard him, and Liz broke up again," Whitney commented of Owen's longtime on-again, off-again girlfriend.

Cassie rolled her eyes. Owen was more of a brother than anything. She had known him all of her life, and there was nothing romantic between them. She doubted there ever could be. He was just too Owen.

The music changed, and a slow song started again. Cassie watched now as several guys all headed over to their table. Some left the dates they came with. Whitney began to laugh as Cassie stared at everyone moving toward them in shock.

"Is this what dances are supposed to be like?" she asked under her breath to her friend. TV school dances never had one girl attracting all the guys.

The younger classman from before pushed the tall senior out of the way as he approached their table. It made Whitney giggle even more, but Cassie couldn't help but gape at them. What the heck was going on?

"Can I—" the younger guy began, but suddenly stopped. He had looked behind Cassie before an arm dropped across her shoulder. "Sorry."

The guy turned on his heels and quickly pushed away back into the approaching crowd. Other guys that had been watching or approaching also left. Cassie turned to the body attached to the familiar arm on her shoulder and smiled up at Owen.

"Figured you could use some help keeping the leeches away," he said while he grinned at Whitney beside Cassie. "Obviously she isn't doing a good enough job to make them leave you alone."

"Hey!" Whitney pouted at him. "She deserves a little fun. Who knows when you'll finally lighten up and let her have some?"

Owen reached forward and grabbed a cookie off Cassie's plate. She swatted at his hand to drop it, but he shoved it all in his mouth in one bite.

"Hey, mister, get your own," Cassie pretend scolded him. Both girls saw Owen as the older-brother type.

"Consider that payment for keeping you safe from all the guys that look like they want to eat you up. You're like Little Red Riding Hood going to see grandma. Don't you know they're all wolves in grandma disguises?" Owen explained.

Cassie rolled her eyes, and Whitney laughed. Owen had always made references to fairy tales since they were small children. Cassie was used to it, but Whitney found it amusing. She had a feeling that was why Owen still told them stuff like that. The music changed to another slow song and people continued to dance and give Cassie glances every now and then, before looking to Owen.

"I'm not sure how much more of this I can take," Cassie told her friends.

"How long is she out of jail?" Owen asked Whitney.

"I made a promise to have her home by midnight," Whitney replied, watching the crowd.

Owen whistled. "Remind me if I ever get in trouble with the law to call your mother. She can argue anything. Wow."

"Yes, good for you, bad for me. Why do you think I still

don't have my own car? She can argue everything," Whitney replied. She had been sulking since she turned sixteen about not getting a car. She was allowed to use her father's car, but Whitney had saved since her first job to buy one herself. Her mother put a stop to that.

"Midnight, like Cinderella?" Owen chuckled, and so did Whitney. "Does that mean she has to stay here until then?"

Whitney smiled. "Nope. I didn't agree to that. I agreed to stay with her until midnight, but not that we would stay in the school."

"Your mom is awesome." Owen held his hand up for a high-five. Whitney hit it.

"What are you guys planning?" Cassie looked between them.

"We plan to take you out on the town since you basically have a 'get out of jail free' pass, at least until your carriage turns back into a pumpkin," Owen explained essentially nothing. "Just don't lose a shoe. You know how Whitney can get about her shoes."

"Just let us change first," Whitney told Owen. "We'll be back in ten."

"Or longer," he added as he pulled their plates in front of himself.

Cassie stood up and followed Whitney around the edge of the dance floor. She was glad her friend didn't plan to walk right through the mass of swaying students. Without Owen close enough, she wasn't sure his overprotective brother act would keep the people away, and she didn't want to get stuck dancing again. She was ready to leave and have fun with her two best friends.

As they neared the darkened doorway of the locker room, Cassie felt her borrowed high heel catch on something on the floor. Owen and his fairy tale jokes had cursed her as her shoe was stuck and ready to come off.

"Whit," Cassie called to her friend, but her voice was covered up by the noise of music blaring somewhere near them.

Whitney continued into the locker room, and Cassie had to precariously bend down to get her shoe out of the wires it was tangled in. A firm grip on her arm balanced her when she almost slipped a second time. It wouldn't have been good to fall down in the dangerously short dress she was wearing. Thankfully, she was hidden in the darkness of the locker room corner, but it still wouldn't be good. Cassie didn't look up at the person helping her, who she could only assume was Owen since he always seemed to come to her rescue.

She slipped out of her shoes. What was the use, anyway? Playing dress up was done. There was no way she could go home in the dress she was wearing, and Whitney and Owen had already planned to take her out somewhere else.

Looking up the arm of the guy balancing her, she finally stood with both shoes in her hands. She let one shoe drop as she tried to cover up her shock. Owen wasn't the one saving her this time. Familiar piercing blue eyes stared at her in the darkness. Holding her arm was Nathaniel Bay.

Cassie didn't know what to say as Nate bent down and retrieved her dropped shoe with his free hand. He smiled at her as she fumbled to take it from him. His warm hand had not left her arm since he helped balance her only moments before.

"As graceful as ever, I see," Nate teased, a smile forming at the corners of his lips.

Cassie didn't know how to respond. At one time, she had been good friends with Nate. She, along with Nate and Owen, had been called the three musketeers for years by everyone. That was until her powers developed and people began to fear her. About the same time, Nate became part of the popular crowd. Since sixth grade, Cassie had only spoken maybe a few words to him in total. He never had approached her. This was a complete first for her.

"Having fun?" he asked, not looking at the room behind

her, but keeping his beautiful blue eyes on her instead.

Cassie didn't know how to respond.

Nate's hand slid down her arm to her waist, never letting go of her as Cassie stood only inches from him. She was more than aware of how close their bodies were as the music changed behind them from a song with a thumping bass to a romantic slow one. It was more than ironic, and even as short as a year ago, Cassie would have been thrilled to be in a dark corner with Nate. She had to remind herself that that was a year ago and not now. He had a girlfriend, and Cassie was way over him. At least she tried to tell herself that.

"I suppose not," Nate replied when she didn't. "You aren't the type that likes to be the center of attention. Glad Owen made it in time to keep the rest of them away."

Cassie bit her lip. She was glad, too, but how he said it seemed odd. *Was he watching what happened?*

"Are you guys heading out to the bonfire?" Nate asked, still not letting go of Cassie.

She hated that he didn't break his hold on her. She couldn't. After years of just wishing he was still her friend, the romantic closeness was more than enough to keep her mind on the fantasy she had tried to convince herself would never be true. Nate wasn't the same guy that had once been her best friend.

Nate glanced down at Cassie when she didn't reply. His baby blue eyes stared openly at her. While she wanted to feel what he was thinking, she stopped herself. She knew enough to not look and get her heart broken. Nate had dated over half a dozen girls in the school the past summer alone. She didn't need to be a sucker for his games and cute looks. That would be easy. And, boy, did Cassie wish she could go with easy.

"I'm sorry everything has changed over the years. Hopefully, you'll find it in your heart to forgive me." Nate was still giving her an open book. "I promise I will make it up to you."

"What?" Cassie finally got a word out. He was making as much sense as the guys—who she didn't know—asking her to dance.

"I'll make it up to you if you let me." Nate leaned in. He was so close the loose hair that usually fell in front of his eyes brushed Cassie's forehead.

Cassie didn't have time to protest or even get a coherent thought together before his lips gently touched hers. She was really kissing Nathaniel Bay in the gym at homecoming. Cassie almost wanted to have an out of body experience to see it herself. Not that she needed that. Nate's hand around her waist held her gently yet firmly to him. It was her first time being let out of the house on a Friday night, her first dance, and now her first kiss. She tried to think of what to do, but she didn't need to—her hands had a mind of their own. Dropping her shoe, she held onto the arms wrapped around her.

Nate pulled back with a triumphant smile. He glanced over her shoulder and shook his head.

"We can talk later at the bonfire. Tell your uncle I'll bring you back afterward," Nate told her before gently releasing her from his arms.

Cassie's head was still spinning. Nate had just kissed her. She wanted to pretend it didn't happen, yet she could still feel his lips on hers. He really had kissed her.

"I've liked you since we were kids, and I'm glad you will be my girlfriend," Nate told her as he proudly gazed at her.

Girlfriend? Cassie was confused, but that word was exactly what was needed to bring her back to reality. And she had said nothing about being his girlfriend. She wasn't even sure why her hands had betrayed her and let him kiss her instead of pushing him away. Okay, she understood that much. He was hot. No one could deny that. But she wasn't about to be the girlfriend of someone who changed girls like a pair of socks. Popular Than, no matter how nice to look at, was just not for her. Old, friendly Nate would have been nice, and was the one she fantasized about, but this version wasn't for her. Besides, Nate already had a girlfriend.

Realization set in. Cassie had just kissed a guy dating someone else. *How could I have done that?* She might not have liked Jess—or was it Shel he was dating now?—but she wasn't about to go around kissing someone else's boyfriend. That was a mistake, and one Cassie wouldn't make again.

"Not even close." Cassie finally found her voice. "You already have a girlfriend."

Nate shrugged like it didn't matter. "She already knew that I didn't plan to stay with her once you passed your exam. She was fun while I was passing time, but since you decided to go and grow up, it's time I do, too."

Yep. This was the Nate Cassie didn't like, and it was a lot easier to walk away from him. Passing time? Who talked about another person that way? Yep, Jerk Nate.

"Sorry, but I'm not your girlfriend, and even if I was allowed to date—which I'm not—I wouldn't choose you," Cassie told Nate. Her hands finally followed her mind's lead and pushed him away as she reached to grab her shoes.

She didn't stop at his shocked face. 'King of the School' Nathaniel Bay had just been turned down. Cassie couldn't believe she actually could do it, but it felt good. She didn't want to be toyed with, and that was all he did now. The nice Nate was gone and had been for a long time. She regretted not pushing him away when he first steadied her from falling. She wouldn't make that mistake twice. No matter how enticing those baby blues were, Cassie wasn't going to be Nate's flavor of the week.

It only took Whitney five minutes to change out of her dress, but Cassie took longer. Owen would be waiting and ready to give her crap about it, but Cassie didn't care. She was slightly lost in her own world of confusion. The dance was strange, and Nate was strange. Wasn't the test supposed to change everything? Wasn't the school and everyone supposed to open their arms and stop all the secrets? Cassie just wanted to be normal.

"Earth to Cas," Whitney said, tapping Cassie's head. "Are you home? Too much loud music ruined your hearing?" Whitney guessed.

"Something like that," Cassie mumbled as she pulled her sweatshirt over her head.

"What did Than want to talk to you about?" Whitney asked.

Than. Yeah, that was Than talking to her. That would be the best way to differentiate between what her heart and head disagreed about. Than was the one talking to her, not the Nate she remembered.

"Something about seeing me at the bonfire," Cassie replied, looking to Whitney for an explanation.

"Yeah, he'll probably be there, but that doesn't matter. You'll have me and Owen to keep you company. You won't have to deal with Than's crowd," Whitney replied. She was almost as overprotective as Owen at times.

"But I probably need to stop by my place to tell my uncle," Cassie added.

She really didn't want to, but Uncle John could smell anything. If he smelled bonfire smoke on her and she had to explain, he would turn into a bear to deal with. It would be easier to just go with them and hope he was asleep for the night, but there was always the chance he would be up or waiting for her to return and catch her. Cassie really didn't want to deal with that. She still didn't know how she was going to tell him about the exam. She hoped Aunt Maria would be home soon. That was the only thing that would save her from his wrath once he found out.

"Ahh, really? Come on. We can lie to him. He'll never know," Whitney protested as she bundled her dress and Cassie's borrowed one back into their white bags before standing to leave.

Cassie untied the updo Whitney had worked so hard to make. She shook her hair loose and grabbed her own book bag to follow Whitney.

"You know how he is. If I don't tell him, he might never let me out again," Cassie replied as they made their way to the locker room door. She wasn't exaggerating, and Whitney knew that.

Whitney reluctantly nodded.

"But he'll say no." Whitney pouted while stepping out into the still-darkened gym and turning to go out the back door.

"Who will say no?" Owen asked from the shadows. Cassie hadn't even noticed him and could barely hear him.

Owen stepped into the dim gym light and waited for a response. Whitney began to leave, and Cassie followed. It was no use talking in the gym with the music going. Outside it was still noisy, but at least Cassie was certain she hadn't lost any hearing from the excessive bass next to the locker room.

Owen stepped in front of Cassie and Whitney to get a reply to his question. He was back in full older brother mode.

"Her uncle," Whitney replied.

The cautious look on Owen's face morphed into a smile.

"Of course he'll say no. That's why we should just go to the party and deal with it later." Owen was also perfectly okay lying to Uncle John. He thought her uncle was more unreasonable than Whitney did and neither had a clue what it was really like to live with Uncle John. "Better to ask forgiveness than permission."

"Not in my house. I don't want to go home afterward and be in trouble. It's fall," Cassie complained as if that explained it all.

Everyone knew John was worse to deal with in fall and spring. Cassie imagined it was some sort of seasonal disorder, but she had yet to find how to treat him for it. If she had, she would slip it into his morning coffee.

"Yes, so let's not tell him," Whitney replied. "It's fall. That means he'll be asleep by the time you get home."

"And if he waits up for me and I come home smelling like a campfire?" Cassie glanced between her two best friends.

They looked at each other, having a silent conversation with their eyes only. Shaking her head, Cassie rolled her eyes at them. There was no way they were going to convince her otherwise. They didn't have to live with John.

"I'll talk to him," Owen finally offered.

"You're going to tell him that you're taking me out into the woods at night, and you think he'll be okay with that?" Cassie asked in disbelief. Very few people would stand up to her uncle, and Owen wasn't one of them.

Owen shrugged. "It's me or Whitney, and I think I have a better chance. Unless Whitney has been taking lessons from her mother, then …" Owen faded off, and Whitney hit him.

"So you think I'm right?" Cassie asked, wondering why they'd both changed their minds.

"No. But you do need a better sweatshirt. It's cold outside if you haven't noticed." Owen began to walk away.

Cassie looked at Whitney, who shrugged. Now, Whitney was one of those that didn't mind standing up to her uncle. But instead, Owen had decided to do it. They were switching places. One more strange thing to add to her day.

Cassie followed Owen outside. He was right. It was colder outside, but that wasn't Cassie's fault. She had planned to just pick up her stuff and go home, not stay at school for hours. Cassie turned to begin walking home when Owen reached out and grabbed her arm.

"I drove over," he explained. They both lived close enough that they walked to school most of the time. She hadn't even thought about driving. "I'll take you back home."

"Oh yeah," Cassie replied, wanting to slap her own

forehead for the lame response.

"Oh yeah," Owen repeated, just to tease her.

"Coming with us?" Cassie asked Whitney.

"Nope, I'll meet you guys there. My mom gave me her car for the night," Whitney explained. Cassie nodded. "I'd give you a kiss, but I don't think our date is done yet," Whitney teased.

"I don't kiss on the first date," Cassie teased back.

They had spent so much time together there once was a false rumor going around that they had something going on the side. Cassie and Whitney didn't care, since it was started by someone they preferred to ignore, but it didn't go over well with Owen. The rumor only got around the school for half a day before he had it stopped. Owen was someone people listened to at school, but talking to her uncle was going to be a first.

Cassie followed Owen to his car in the parking lot. She didn't need him to show her where it was—you couldn't miss the chipped lime green paint job he had tried to do himself the summer before. Art wasn't one of his strong points.

"You really want to talk to Uncle John?" Cassie asked, as she shut the door and turned all the vents to herself. She didn't have a coat with her, and it was much chillier than she expected. She would be grabbing a sweatshirt, and maybe even some mittens, before going to the bonfire if she was let out of her prison.

"Want to? Heck no. I know as well as anyone he isn't fun to deal with, but you shouldn't have to stay home all the time. He's way too protective," Owen replied, driving away from the school and honking at Whitney as they passed her getting into her car. Cassie wanted to laugh. Owen was almost as protective as her uncle.

"And what if he says no?" That was actually not exactly how she pictured it, but it was better than telling Owen he would be lucky to get out of the house without a black eye for asking. 'Overprotective' was an understatement with Uncle John.

"Then we will have to just sit around your house playing video games," Owen replied. "But don't worry. I can be persuasive, too."

He wiggled his eyebrows. Cassie had to laugh. Persuasive wasn't one of his qualities.

"Sure," Cassie replied as Owen gave a quick right turn after the sudden left turn. It wasn't sudden because Cassie knew where they were going but more so sudden because Owen was speeding through a yellow, almost red, light.

It didn't even take five minutes to make it to her house. Hopping out, Cassie wondered if she should just send Owen home. She had already had the longest time away from home that she could remember in close to forever, she didn't need to go out again. However, telling Owen to leave wasn't an option as he got out and hurried to the front door. He let himself in before Cassie could stop him, as if she would send him home if they waited even a moment longer.

"Is that you, Cassie?" John yelled from the family room in the back of the house.

"Yeah, and Owen," Cassie replied, giving Owen a look that said *go away*.

"Came home early?" he asked from his spot in the Lazy Boy recliner chair he sat in most of the time.

"Actually, sir, we came home to get warmer clothes," Owen replied, bravely stepping up to tell Cassie's uncle they were going out.

"Warmer clothes?" John asked, eyebrow raised. He actually looked a little amused that Owen would speak to him.

"Cassie wanted to go with Whitney and me to the fire tonight," Owen added quickly, spitting out the words almost too fast to understand them.

John jumped up from his chair, quicker than Cassie expected.

"No way," John replied, standing to his full height, which was inches above Owen.

For his part, Owen was being quite brave. He attempted to stand eye-to-eye with John and didn't back down. That wasn't a scene Cassie saw often. John was intimidating lying in his chair; standing, he was beyond intimidating. His massive upper body was twice the width of a normal-sized person and his unruly brown, almost black, hair that needed cutting gave him additional height. But for all the physicality that made her uncle imposing, it was his eyes that you didn't want to look into. He was outright scary.

"She doesn't go to the fires. The Council of Elders agreed to that. You know the rules," John told Owen, his eyes blazing in an unspoken challenge.

Normally Owen wouldn't have been that brave, but now he didn't even shrink away.

"The rule was she didn't get to mingle with everyone until she joined the coven. I don't think anyone is going to mind now that she passed her apprentice test yesterday."

Cassie's mouth dropped open. She hadn't planned to tell her uncle this soon, but even so, Owen was being so brash. She was going to let Uncle John know once he was well fed and in a happy mood. You didn't tell the giant bear that was her uncle things that bluntly.

"What?" Uncle John roared, and Owen finally backed away from the older man, keeping Cassie behind himself.

Cassie wanted to run away, but John turned his full gaze to her. His anger was more than evident in his red face. She didn't need to see his eyes to know he was beyond upset.

"You did what?" he asked, his face burning as he tried to rein in his anger.

Cassie was speechless as she watched the vein in his forehead bulge. One thing Uncle John was very good at was hearing everything. She didn't need to repeat herself.

"She didn't want me to tell you, but I knew you wouldn't let her go otherwise." Owen was able to talk again at least.

He sent an 'I'm sorry' to Cassie with his eyes. He wasn't going to be forgiven for a long time in Cassie's book. She stared back at him sourly.

"Not possible. She couldn't have taken the exam. You need permission from your guardian to do that," John replied, keeping his anger only slightly in check. "I'm your guardian, and I sure as heck didn't give you permission to do anything like that."

"The exact wording is your parents' permission," Cassie squeaked out. John was terrifying to look at, even if he hadn't yet broken furniture or the walls as it often came to with his unchecked anger.

John glared at Cassie. "I'm your guardian," he repeated slowly, blowing a breath out between each word.

"But my parents are dead," Cassie added. It was a low blow to be so blunt, but she had no other way of telling him. Yes, Owen was now on her bad list. It would have gone much better if she had time to come up with a way to tell her uncle.

John's anger instantly softened. "We don't know that. Your mother might still be alive." John hadn't given up hope as everyone else had.

"No. Both of them must be dead because they said that I wouldn't have been able to do the exam if either my father or mother were alive and didn't give me permission." Cassie stared at the floor. She knew how bad it felt when she found out the truth; she hated that not only did she go behind her uncle's back, but now she had to tell him the truth about her mother.

"That can't be true," John tried to deny everything.

Cassie didn't want it to be true either. But she had read the coven rules many times. She needed parental permission. That was the only requirement for taking the exam.

"Cassie, may I?" Owen asked, finally speaking. He motioned to Cassie's hair. She gave him an odd look but bobbed her head yes.

36

Owen turned Cassie's back to her uncle and lifted up her hair. John sucked in his breath.

"What?" Cassie asked, turning to look at her now-stunned uncle.

"When you join the coven there's a mark that forms on the back of your neck. That's the proof that you passed your exam," Owen explained what he had done.

"But you said she just did it," John finally spoke. "How could she have chosen a mate already?"

"What?" Owen asked, reaching back and lifting up Cassie's hair again, this time looking behind her also.

"What?" Cassie repeated what Owen had said as she turned and saw his slight smile drop.

"When did you have time alone with Than?" Owen asked, his calm demeanor turning into anger.

"Than?" Cassie replied. What were they talking about?

"Than? As in Nathaniel Bay?" John asked, not explaining what was going on either, but obviously upset at something.

"Yeah. That's Than's mark," Owen added, sulking a bit.

"What's Than's mark?" Cassie looked between her uncle and friend.

"Can it be undone?" Owen asked John, hope lingering in his voice.

John shook his head. "She's already proved that she doesn't need my approval for anything. She's made her choice. That's that." John dejectedly sat back down in his chair. His anger was all gone now, and he was back in his normal hibernation spot.

"Choice about what?" Cassie asked.

They had thrown around the word mate and Than in the same breath. She didn't like the sound of that, just as she hadn't liked Nate declaring she would be his girlfriend without asking her. Cassie looked at Owen, but he was already staring at the doorway. She turned to her uncle, but he was just as disagreeable.

"Take her to the fire. Maybe she can see what she's

getting into because she isn't my problem any longer," John grabbed the remote as he laid back.

Cassie knew him well enough to know that it was just words. He loved his sister greatly, and the news that she was truly gone was going to take a long time for him to adjust to. Cassie wanted to miss her parents as much as he did, but she never knew them. She was angrier at being left alone than sad at finding out the truth.

"Let's go," Owen said, he already was turned to the door.

She gave her uncle one last look. She probably should have stayed to keep him company, but her curiosity of finding out any of the town secrets was too appealing. John seemed to think she would learn more at the bonfire. She had to hope so since no one had let her in on the secrets yet.

Cassie hurried outside behind Owen. He didn't even pause to see if she were following. She slid into the passenger seat of his car and studied him as he pulled out of the driveway. She could tell he was still silently angry.

"What's going on? What did I do?" Cassie asked. Wasn't *she* the one that was supposed to be angry? Owen had told her uncle about her exam when she had asked him not to. He had broken *her* trust.

Owen stopped at the end of the driveway and looked at Cassie.

"He really didn't say anything to you?" Owen cautiously asked. The anger was replaced by hurt now. Something was going on, and she had no clue.

"Who said what? You guys are confusing," she complained. Cassie rubbed her forehead before pulling her fingers through her hair to detangle the crunchy curls.

"Did you agree to…" Owen paused and thought for a moment. "Did you agree to date him?"

Cassie laughed. It had to be a joke. Owen, as well as everyone else, knew that Cassie couldn't date, let alone would she date Nate. He was part of the popular crowd, not even close to what she was looking for in a guy. Owen didn't laugh. He was still serious.

"No," she replied. "Besides, he has a girlfriend. Why are you worried?"

Owen let out the breath he was holding. He smiled as he blew his dishwater blond hair off his forehead. His mood changed instantly.

"Maybe there's hope after all," he said under his breath as he whipped out onto the street and headed north out of town.

CHAPTER 3

Cassie arrived at James Park with Owen in a much better mood. She could almost say he was back to himself, but she would have been lying. He was still slightly distant, and she had no clue why. They had been best friends since they were little. She didn't want that to ever change; especially over something they had said she'd done, but hadn't.

Cassie slipped out of the car into the dark in the parking lot. James Park really wasn't the kind of park with a swing set and slide. It was more like a wooded area with a large stone open shelter that people would use to throw parties at. It was beautiful in the summer when all the flowers were blooming in the surrounding woods, and down by the large lake. Cassie loved to hike all the adjoining trails, but in the cold, now slightly wet fall, it had lost some of its appeal. That was until she passed the shelter and saw the fire blazing down by the lake.

The ground was slippery as it was, but when Cassie didn't notice the branch sticking out of the pathway, she was thankful that Owen was back to being her friend. His arm quickly rushed out and caught her before she took a face-plant into the earthen pathway. Normally, Cassie wouldn't mind—she loved nature and everything outside—but it was her first time being allowed out to the bonfire, and she didn't want to show up covered in mud. She decided it was best to hold onto Owen, who seemed to have no trouble leading the way down to the lake in the dark.

As the fire grew brighter, she began to notice all the people lounging around. She had thought that there would only be a few people since the dance was still going on, but there were a lot more than she expected. Whitney had talked about the lake bonfires before, and she had made it seem like not that big of a deal. Cassie saw now as more people rushed past her and Owen that it was slightly a big deal. There were more people at the lake than the dance.

"I think Whitney's over there," Owen said, pointing toward their waiting friend.

They stepped into the sand, and Cassie didn't want to drop her hold on Owen. He grinned as she grasped his arm tighter. A muddy impression wouldn't be good, but falling on the uneven sand would be just as bad.

Owen led the way through several groups of students that sat around. Cassie could still see the same divisions as there were in school. Each group of friends was divided from the rest, but at least here they were a little more mashed together to be near the warm fire.

"You guys actually made it!" Whitney cheered when Owen finally reached her. "I was beginning to think John wouldn't let you come."

"He wasn't going to, but Owen convinced him to let me." Cassie gave Owen all the credit he deserved for facing John.

Whitney wiggled her eyebrows at Owen, and he swatted at her.

"He had to let her. She's part of all this now, why would he make her stay away? He had no reason," Owen replied like it was nothing.

"Whatever," Whitney said. She knew it was a big deal to stand up to John. "Can you go get us some drinks, so we don't have to get cold and leave the fire?"

Owen nodded, and Cassie dropped down to sit next to Whitney.

"I can't believe he actually let you out. This is awesome," Whitney added.

Cassie had to agree. First, he allowed her to go to a dance, and now the bonfire. Cassie should have taken the exam years ago. It still was bit confusing, but at least she fit in a bit more than normal.

"John and Owen got into some argument about me coming, and something was said about me choosing a mate. What the heck was that about?" Cassie asked Whitney.

Whitney began to cough as she inhaled her gum. Cassie quickly patted her on the back before someone who hadn't been sitting too far away turned and smacked her harder than Cassie ever could have. The piece of gum flew out of her mouth and into the fire.

"That's not possible. You haven't been out of my sight long enough to mate with anyone," Whitney added.

Cassie scrunched up her face in confusion.

"That came out wrong. What I mean is that you couldn't have chosen a mate. It takes a bit more time than just having a crush on someone. And if you had, I would have known when I was doing your hair."

"You mean this?" Cassie asked, rubbing the back of her neck. She still didn't feel anything there, and when she had peeked in the mirror as they rushed out of the house, she didn't see anything.

"Yeah that," Whitney replied, she hadn't seen it, but she knew what Cassie walk talking about.

Cassie brushed her hair back as if she could see behind her head.

"What the …" Whitney added as she stopped Cassie's hand from releasing the hair she had picked up.

"Yeah, isn't that interesting?" Owen said as he finally arrived back to their spot. He had three drinks in his hand. He gave one to each of them, while keeping one for himself, and then sat down next to Cassie.

"Nathaniel Bay? I swear that wasn't there before the dance," Whitney told Owen, almost like she was apologizing.

"Okay, someone better explain." Cassie glanced between her two best friends who sat on either side of her. "Why do you guys keep mentioning Nate?"

Whitney looked to Owen, and he shrugged. He didn't seem to be any more forthcoming than at Cassie's house or the ride to the party. When would the secrets be over?

"She's part of everything now, right?" Whitney asked. Owen shrugged. He didn't have an answer. "This is frustrating. Either she's one of us or not. How can they not know?"

Cassie stared at her friend. She didn't know if she was supposed to answer because she didn't have a reply. A second look told Cassie that Whitney didn't seem to be talking to anyone in particular as she let off some pent-up frustration.

"I don't know. John didn't seem to know either," Owen replied. For once, Cassie wasn't the only one confused.

"But she passed her exam, and she's already marked. How can she not be one of us?" Whitney was beyond frustrated now.

Cassie rolled her eyes. Everyone seemed to think talking in code was better than not telling her. It wasn't. She still felt left out. Most of the time, Whitney and Owen were better at not discussing things around her, but she could feel the frustration Whitney felt.

"Fine. We can't tell her everything yet, but we can tell her bits." Whitney turned to Cassie and paused with her finger on her lips as she thought.

"As long as it's in general terms, no one can get in trouble, right?" Owen was searching for a way to tell Cassie also.

"Agreed? Tell me something," Cassie begged.

"Once you join the coven, you get to choose your mate," Whitney replied. Owen's eyes bugged out at how much Whitney was saying. "Hey. That's general enough to not get us into trouble. She's already part way there, so they can't get mad about that. And if she has a mate, she ought to know what that means."

43

"Mate?" Cassie asked. She knew what it meant in animal terms, but there wasn't a single person who used that word as much as she had heard it in the last thirty minutes.

"Essentially your husband," Whitney replied, shrugging her answer.

"Husband?" Cassie asked in shock. "Um, did you hit your head or something? We're only sixteen."

Whitney shrugged again. "Seventeen in a few months, and in the coven that's plenty old to get ..."

"Married," Owen supplied before Whitney added more.

"And you guys think I chose my mate already?" Cassie couldn't even say his name out loud. It was crazy. She didn't even like Nate, let alone want to marry him. They might not have cared that she was only sixteen, but she cared. She had a lot more life to live before deciding to marry someone.

Owen turned to the fire and shrugged.

"The mark on your neck says you chose Nate and he chose you," Whitney explained what Owen wouldn't.

Cassie stared in disbelief between her two friends. They were serious about it. It had to be a joke.

"Ha, ha, you guys. How'd you get John to play along?" Cassie asked. Marriage at seventeen. It was crazy, and she almost believed them.

Whitney looked at her and shook her head as Owen stared wide-eyed at her.

"Really. How'd he ever agree? Wait. Don't tell me. Was it part of taking me out? Were you supposed to scare me into never asking to go out again?" Cassie kept talking though her friends didn't respond. She glanced between them, but there was no laughter in their expressions.

"Sorry, hon, this isn't a joke," Whitney finally replied.

"Sure. We all should get married at seventeen. Sounds like a great age. Uncle John won't even let me date, yet you want me to believe you that he'll let me get married? And to Nate of all people? You guys know that I don't like him anymore. That crush was back in grade school." Cassie realized her friends still weren't laughing, and she got a little nervous it might not be a joke.

"It isn't John's choice whether you marry or not," Owen replied.

"True. That should be my choice, and why would I choose Nate? You mean the friend that ditched us to be popular? Not a chance in …" Cassie added but stopped when her neck left a weird tingling sensation going down her back. She turned in time to see Nate arrive at the beach with several of his buddies.

"How can that happen if she doesn't even know? Isn't it supposed to be a decision they both make; otherwise every guy would go around marking the girl he wanted. This can't be right."

Cassie turned to find Whitney whispering to Owen.

"You guys still trying to play up that whole mating crap?" Cassie asked. Owen and Whitney shot each other looks. "Okay. Fine. I'll play along. Not like I haven't seen weirder stuff with all the witches. Especially the—" Cassie stopped. She wasn't supposed to say anything about the other witches called the sidhe, but it was getting harder and harder to do so. She was just happy she had told Whitney.

"Let's pretend that you believe us," Whitney started as she looked across the fire to where Nate sat with his friends.

"Sure," Cassie replied, watching across the fire also, though she didn't want to. She couldn't help it. Nate had to pick a spot exactly across the fire from them.

"Did you talk to Than tonight?" Whitney asked.

"Kind of. He stopped me before we went to get changed. He said I could be his girlfriend, and I told him no," Cassie added, looking between her friends. How in the world was that a *Yes, I want to marry you?*

"See. I told you she wouldn't be stupid enough to agree to tricks," Whitney added to Owen.

"You told him no?" Owen asked again.

"I think my exact words were along the lines that even if

I were allowed to date, I would never choose him," Cassie replied, trying not to look across the fire to the glowing blue eyes of Nate that seemed to be taking in everything.

"Then how does she have his mark?" Whitney asked.

"That's exactly what I want to know," Owen replied, more than frustrated.

"Can we just forget about that stuff and enjoy the fact I was let out of my prison for a couple hours?" Cassie asked, trying to change the subject. She still felt they were waiting for the punch line to make her laugh, but the longer they held out, the more it worried her. Did she want to be let in on all the secrets if everyone was going to talk about strange stuff?

"Exactly," Owen said, raising his glass as if to toast and clunking it to Cassie's in her hand.

Cassie took a large sip and then sputtered on it as it burned her throat.

"What is this stuff?" Cassie gave her cup to Owen. She wasn't going to drink any more of it.

"Trust me, you don't want to know," Whitney replied, gulping down her own drink.

Cassie immediately felt lightheaded, and the bit of magic she tasted as she drank made her even drowsier.

"Cas, you all right?" Owen asked, concern lacing his voice.

"I think I'm just going to rest my head," Cassie replied, leaning on Owen's shoulder.

Whitney patted her head.

"I've heard of lightweights before, but one drink is a bit funny," Whitney added.

Owen shifted to let Cassie rest better against his arm.

"Do you think that the mark is permanent?" Whitney asked after some time. She assumed Cassie was out of it.

"I hope not," Owen replied. He pulled Cassie closer as she tried not to drift off to sleep.

"Because you've been an idiot and waited too long to tell her how much you love her?" Whitney replied.

Now Cassie wished she could force her eyes open to see if what Whitney was saying was true. She never suspected Owen liked her. He had never been anything but friendly with her. Sure, he was always there to help her whenever she needed it, but it was what friends were like. He was her friend.

Cassie felt herself melt even farther against Owen's shoulder as her body shut down. She felt paralyzed even though her mind was completely awake. Cassie felt the magic swirl in her blood. She knew better than to drink anything she hadn't seen someone make. Why had she been stupid?

Without speaking, Cassie began to think about the words she needed to undo the magic binding down her body. She didn't have anything with her to strengthen the spell, but if she could at least get her mouth moving, it would be a start. Cassie repeated the words in her mind another two times. Tingles were beginning to form. Cassie repeated the words again. Whoever did it was good, but not good enough to stop Cassie's magic.

"Maaa," Cassie got the syllable out, but she needed a few more rounds to counter-curse the magic in her.

"What?" Owen asked.

Whitney picked up Cassie's arm. She tapped her hand a few times and gently placed it back down.

"Who'd you get the drink from?" Whitney asked. Her words sounded a bit mushed to Cassie, but she listened in anyway.

"Jess was handing them out, why?" Owen replied. He took Cassie's hand and tapped it also. Still no response. Cassie wasn't even trying to get her hands back.

"As in Jess, Than's newly dumped girlfriend?" Whitney scolded.

"Shit," Owen dumped all three glasses on the ground.

"Wait. A. Second." Cassie tried to think straight and took a breath between each word. All other muscle control was gone. She couldn't open her eyes as she felt two strong arms lift her into the air.

"We need to get her out of here and find the antidote before her uncle finds out. He would kill me if he knew I gave her a drink that was laced," Owen quickly told Whitney.

She mumbled some sort of agreement as she stood and her keys jingled.

"Why would Jess do this?" Cassie got out her question even though her eyes wouldn't open.

No one replied, but her knight in shining armor who was whisking her away began to walk through the dark woods. Even if she could open her eyes, Cassie wouldn't see anything. First Owen had to hold her hand to help her walk through the woods, and now he had to carry her home. He sure did earn his spot as her best friend. It didn't matter. Her epic jailhouse break was a bust anyway. At least she still had Owen to save her. He sat her inside his car before going around and starting up the engine. Cassie could feel the car start moving.

It was a shorter drive than she remembered, but on the way over she had spent the whole time worrying about Owen. Something seemed off. But at least now, aside from the silent treatment, he was back to his old self. Cassie felt her door open, and she hoped they were at Whitney's house. She couldn't go home all magicked up and hope that Uncle John would ever let her out again.

Since she couldn't move, Cassie waited for Owen to press a bottle to her lips. At least she had her mouth moving again and could swallow. Owen took her hands in his, and she could feel the warmth from them. His hands felt softer than she remembered, but then again she wasn't completely in control of herself.

Cassie felt the potion Owen had given her wake every muscle in her body back up. The tingles hit her all over at once, and she wanted to itch them. It was like how a foot feels waking up from falling asleep times ten. Jess wasn't a very powerful witch, but she sure knew what she was doing. Would she even apologize when Cassie went to school Monday, and Jess found out that Cassie had no intention of dating Nate? Somehow Cassie doubted it.

"Do you feel better now?" a voice that wasn't Owen's asked.

Cassie slowly cracked open her eyes. She already knew that voice. She closed her eyes again and wished she could change who was only inches away from her, staring into her face. Cassie opened her eyes again, and it was still him. Nate's blue eyes were watching her with worry.

"**Where are my** friends?" Cassie asked, feeling stupid that she had thought it was Owen all along.

"I told them that you're my responsibility, so I would be taking you home," Nate replied. This wasn't what Cassie heard.

Cassie wished she had the strength to glare at him, but instead kept her eyes closed. She wasn't his responsibility. She wasn't anyone's responsibility but her own. One of the first things every young witch learns is not to drink anything that you didn't see made.

"Do you think you can walk?" Nate asked. They were parked outside her house.

Cassie shook her head, and Nate automatically scooped her up into his arms as if she weighed nothing. Cassie wanted to beat against his chest to make him let go, but everything was still tingling, and any movement made it worse.

"Put me down," Cassie finally said as they neared the doorway. Nate looked at her doubtfully, but she put her best serious face on to try to convince him. When he gingerly set her on the top step tingles shot up her legs.

"Don't worry. Jess will be dealt with," Nate told Cassie.

That hadn't actually occurred to her. Yeah, getting laced with a potion sucked, but it wasn't that bad. Cassie had felt worse. She had been hit by a blast over the summer by a sidhe witch that could cast real magic, not the practice stuff Jess was using. *That* really hurt. This was just a minor inconvenience. It probably would have taken Cassie at least twenty minutes, but she could have undone everything on her own eventually. No, Jess was the furthest thing from her mind. Cassie was much more worried about everything else. Plopping down on the step, she attempted to catch her breath.

First off, why did her friends ditch her with Nate? That wasn't like Owen, and especially not something Whitney would do. She already explained she wasn't dating Nate, and had no plans to. Did her friends not believe her? Secondly, she was returning from a party with magic on and in her. Her uncle was going to be furious. He hated when Cassie had to practice magic in the house for school. He wasn't going to like her coming home smelling like it. Even if he wasn't a witch and couldn't feel magic as one, he still had a great sense about it. While other classmates could change their hair color with a spell, Cassie was never allowed to do magic like that. Her uncle had forbidden any magic in the house without his approval. She wasn't so sure she wanted to go inside. He might just kick her out like he threatened.

"You need to rest," Nate told her as he reached down to help her stand.

Cassie brushed off his hands and Nate looked shocked.

"What is all this stuff about your mark and claiming me? I'm pretty sure I made it clear I don't plan to date you," Cassie told him, pushing herself to an unassisted, yet wobbly stand.

"What do you mean?" he asked, like he didn't understand what she was saying.

"I am not your girlfriend." Cassie tried to enunciate as best she could. Jess' anger was easy enough to feel with her magic still resonating through her blood.

"Of course not," Nate replied. Cassie sighed in relief that at least they could agree on that. "You're my mate."

Cassie couldn't stop her mouth from dropping open. He seemed oblivious of her choice.

"I wouldn't date you if you paid me." Cassie reached for the door handle to let herself in. She'd rather deal with John's wrath over unapproved magic than Nate and his delusion that there was something more between them.

Surprise laced Nate's eyes.

"You already chose me, why this game now?" Nate asked. "Anyone else would feel lucky to be you, and here you are complaining. I don't get you, Cas."

A pang of sadness hit Cassie when he used the nickname he had called her in grade school, but she didn't let that change her mind. Nate had always been charismatic, even back then. He could get just about anyone to do anything he wanted. Cassie wasn't immune to his charms, but he never asked her to do anything that would get her in trouble, unlike Owen and Nate. They were in trouble all the time. Cassie was always the good girl. She did what was asked of her and never asked questions. She wasn't going to be that Cassie anymore. She wanted answers, not someone bossing her around. She got enough of that from John.

Cassie opened the door and slid inside, only opening it wide enough for her body to slip through. She tried to shut the door on Nate, but his foot was quicker than hers, with her not quite awake muscles. Nate reached forward and quickly grabbed Cassie's arm before she could make it away.

"We need to talk," he whispered to her. "But not here."

Cassie wanted to protest, but Nate already had her back out the door and quickly shut it much more quietly than she had opened it. Nate let go of her arm, and Cassie stopped right at the top of the stairs as he was walking away.

"Not here," he said as he looked at the house.

Cassie was tempted to look behind her and see which

window Uncle John was peering out of, but she didn't. She just stood and watched Nate as he went back to his car. He stopped his car and glanced back at her.

He asked the only question that would be tempting enough to get her to move. "You want answers?"

Cassie begrudgingly followed him. He stood still and didn't get into his car until she sat down and shut the door. Quickly, Nate followed and gracefully slid into his seat. He turned the car on just as fast and sped off away from her uncle's house. Nate didn't drive far before stopping at a park Cassie used to visit as a child. Nate pulled into the parking lot and got out. Cassie had no choice but to follow.

Nate walked over to the swings and sat down. Cassie stood and watched him. He didn't speak but waited for her to sit, too.

"Take you back a few years?" Nate asked as Cassie dangled her feet over the sand.

Cassie had a head full of memories at that particular park with Nate and Owen. Nothing recent, though.

"You said you'd have answers," Cassie replied, getting to business. She was sick of all the games.

"And I do. I just don't know where to start."

"How about the beginning?" Cassie suggested, pushing back and making her swing go a little.

"Were you always this blunt?" Nate moved his own swing a little to keep a slow pace with hers.

"Were you always a jerk who dumps girlfriends for a girl that doesn't even want to date you?"

"Touché," Nate replied with a chuckle.

"So are we here to swing, or do you actually fear my uncle just like everyone else?" Cassie added. It wasn't fear she sensed from Nate earlier, but that was a good excuse to use anyway.

"Do you know anything about your parents?" Nate asked, ignoring her snarkiness.

"They're dead. What else is there to know? They left me

with an uncle that doesn't want me. That just about covers it." Cassie shrugged. There was always more beyond that, but since no one would tell her anything, she had to go with what she knew.

"Dead?" Nate asked, as shocked as Uncle John had been.

Cassie bit her lip. That was a secret she had just told her uncle, too. She had done well to keep it hidden for the weeks leading to the exam. Oh well. It didn't matter, or change anything. It wasn't like Cassie had hoped they would come save her from the crappy town she was being raised in full of people that would point, stare, and talk about her behind her back. She gave up that hope long ago.

"My parents figured that much, but I think my mother was still hoping your mom would show up at some point," Nate replied, staring at the playset that was lit by the bright, almost full, moon in the sky.

Cassie bit her tongue. She forgot that Nate's mother and her mother had been best friends growing up. If anyone still hoped that her mother would return alive someday, it was his mother.

"Has your uncle told you anything about your father?" Nate tested the waters with questions.

Cassie shrugged. Uncle John had told her nothing about, including a name for, her father. The only thing she knew was the baby blanket she had been brought in had an F on it. That meant nothing to anyone in town, and even the most powerful witches couldn't use it to locate her parents.

"What has the coven taught you about the people in town?" Nate asked, changing his questioning but still not making any sense or giving Cassie any answers.

"That we come from a long line of humans that practice magic," Cassie replied. Even Nate had heard that same lecture.

Nate jumped up from his swing and began to pace in the sand before Cassie as he mumbled to himself. She couldn't hear what he was saying, but it was fun to watch him frustrated. Cool and collected Nate Bay was actually at a loss for words. Finally, he stopped his pacing and looked up at Cassie, his eyes reflecting the moon were almost glowing in the dark evening light.

"You never heard anyone mention that there are two types of humans?" Nate asked. His eyes were staring intently at her, waiting for her to answer, which she did not. "Night humans and day humans?"

Now Cassie wondered if maybe she hit her head when she passed out before. She was pretty sure it was just a muscle-relaxing potion, but maybe she did pass out. He wasn't making much sense.

"Witches are day humans. In fact, the witches that live around here are the only day humans that can do magic," Nate continued to explain. Now Cassie was finding him harder to believe. She had met the sidhe. She had seen them do magic, not that she could tell him that.

"Okay. Let's say I believe you. Then what are these night humans?" Cassie asked. Everyone was a bit confusing lately, but Nate was the icing on the cake. He sounded even nuttier than Owen and Whitney with their *mate* talk.

"You know all those horror movies that are always in the theaters?"

Cassie nodded, having no idea where he was going with the change in subject. Not that it mattered. He was talking nonsense anyway.

"Those bad guys that run around killing people and drinking their blood?"

Cassie nodded again, waiting for the punch line. She loved a good horror movie like the next person, but they were getting really off topic now.

"The witches in town make up the day humans, but the rest of us are all night humans. Also known as the blood-drinking bad guys," Nate explained, looking directly at her as he talked.

Cassie's heartbeat picked up. She now regretted not

telling her uncle she was home. She was alone in a park with someone that kind of just admitted he was into drinking blood. Yeah, she had seen those horror movies. Normally the nut jobs like that killed those they lured off alone into the dark of the night. Why hadn't she brought anything with her? She rarely left the house without a bit of magic. She had been too trusting that Owen would stay with her. Where was her knight in shining armor now? He had left her alone with the crazy guy in front of her.

"Cas," Nate said quietly, "I didn't mean to scare you."

Cassie glanced up. He was now closer to her. His eyes were filled with concern, but her heart kept beating fast. He stood back and watched her, waiting for something. His dark, almost black, hair was messily pushed off his forehead from running his hands through it as he talked. His lopsided smile was gone, and a line of worry replaced it. He stood back, not making any sudden moves or anything that was even remotely threatening. Her heartbeat slowed a bit. It was Nate, after all. He could be a jerk, but he wasn't a murderer. At least she had to hope not.

"You've always wanted to know what the big secret was. That's it," Nate told her. He kept his distance, his gaze never leaving hers.

"So half the town likes to drink blood?"

Cassie stared at him in disbelief. He wasn't making a move toward her, but just stood there waiting. He seemed sane, and even had a serious expression on his face like he believed what he was saying. Cassie quickly glanced around to find who was taping their conversation. It had to be a joke.

"Where are Owen and Whitney hiding? And how did you get Jess in on it? Gosh, that's a great girlfriend. How much did they pay you?" Cassie asked, still searching the park in the dark of the night. They had to be hidden well.

"No one paid me anything, and this isn't a joke," Nate replied, taken aback by her change in attitude. "I'm being serious."

"Just like they were serious when they told me all that *mate* crap before?" Cassie asked.

There was no way possible people were running around town getting married at seventeen or drinking blood for that matter. That was all crazy, and probably one of Owen's wild ideas to prank her.

"Mate crap?" Nate asked, seemingly offended.

"Yeah, all that stuff about you and me essentially being married. Nice joke, you guys, but this is taking things a bit far," Cassie said it loudly, so her friends—wherever they were hiding—could hear her.

Nate seemed confused as he looked around the park also.

"Who are you talking to? No one's here," he told her.

"Sure. My friends just left me with you," Cassie replied. They would never do that.

"I told them to leave, and they did. As the next in line to be alpha they have to listen," Nate replied, still perplexed.

"Sure." Cassie stood and squinted into the darkness, searching for her friends. "Well, it's been fun, but I'm tired, and I don't want to miss curfew. I'll have to scold them later for doing this. Cinderella has to go home now," she added rather loudly, hoping wherever Owen was, he would hear her and come out.

Nate followed behind Cassie as she began to walk away.

"Where are you going?" he asked, jumping in front of her to make her stop.

"Home," she replied, like it was obvious. Cassie walked around him and kept going.

"We can go back and pick up your stuff, but really my house is completely stocked," Nate told her as he moved beside her. "I think my mother has been shopping for years, hoping that I'd find a mate. She really wanted a daughter, you know. I think she has hundreds of outfits in almost every size she could find."

Cassie stopped.

"Stocked for what?" That made absolutely no sense.

Nate was being strange as ever, but at least it wasn't any different than normal. Life had always been bewildering for Cassie. Seemed her friends had a sense of humor about it with their prank. She'd thought passing her exam would let her into the group, but now she didn't care. The town could keep their secret games.

"For you to move in," Nate replied, like it was obvious.

"Um. Thanks, but I think you're taking this joke a bit too far." Cassie slowly backed away from him. He might not be the murderer she'd briefly thought he was moments before, but he was still acting odd.

"This isn't a joke. You are my mate."

"Sure," she said slowly, continuing to walk toward the street. "And I'll be the next Queen of Sheba."

Nate paused. "If that's what you want, we can probably arrange something."

Cassie stared at him. He was serious. She wasn't, but now it was getting too weird even for her.

"Well, thanks, but no thanks. I'll just be on my way. You don't know what John can be like when I don't follow his orders," Cassie told him as she continued to walk, keeping an eye on Nate.

"Like a bear?" Nate replied.

Cassie nodded. That was the perfect description of him but why Nate would say that was beyond her.

Opening his car door, Nate slid inside, then reached across the seat and threw open the passenger side door. Cassie didn't trust him—he had been talking strangely.

"Get in. We'll go to your place if you insist before heading back to mine," Nate ordered her.

Cassie wrinkled her nose. She had spent her whole life being ordered around by her uncle. She put up with it because he was her guardian. She wasn't about to be bossed around by someone her own age, no matter what he thought he could do.

"No thanks. I can make it back on my own," Cassie replied. The park was only a few blocks away from her house.

"Cassie, it's night out. Come on. Just get in my car," Nate told her as he started the engine.

Ignoring him, Cassie crossed the street instead. She began walking down the sidewalk before Nate realized that she wasn't about to listen to him.

"Cassie," Nate said from his car as he drove down the street with his window open and car door flopping around. He matched her pace with his car. "Get in the car."

"Yeah. I don't know who you think you are. You might be cute and have tons of people willing to do anything you say, but I'm not one of them," Cassie explained as she kept walking. It was warming her up to walk, so she kept up her brisk pace.

"You have no idea what's out at nighttime. It isn't safe to just walk around." Nate scolded, "Cassandra Aisling Booth, get in the car."

Cassie rolled her eyes. Uncle John didn't even use her full name when yelling at her. Nate was acting like he was her mother.

"If you're worried about me being out a night, you shouldn't have dragged me off to the park to play a prank on me," Cassie replied. "Go home, Nate."

Turning, Cassie cut through the closest yard, knowing the neighbors on her street wouldn't mind her going through their yards. Nate was going to have to go around the block to get to her house at the end of the cul-de-sac. Cassie didn't care if he tried to continue following her—she was going home, and there was nothing he could do to stop her. She couldn't wait to get back home and to her cell phone she had left in her room. Perfectly planned as it was, her friends needed to be chewed out for this prank.

CHAPTER 4

Cassie couldn't get a hold of either Owen or Whitney when she got home, but it didn't matter. She was tired and fell asleep the moment her head hit her pillow. She had gone to her first dance, a bonfire, and even had a spell put on her. It had been an exhausting night. The only reason she got up the next morning was because her growling stomach had woken her up.

She slipped on a sweatshirt—her room was toasty, but John kept the rest of the house freezing—and made her way silently downstairs. Cassie had gotten very good over the years at being quiet. John liked his sleep almost as much as he liked his food in the fall. Nate had been right about one thing: the more she thought about it, the more John could easily have been a bear in another life.

Cassie paused in shock. There were voices coming from the kitchen. Cassie kept to creeping just as silently as she had on the stairs while she continued down the hallway. The living room couch had blankets thrown across it like someone had slept there. That was odd for her uncle. He wasn't the type that needed or wanted blankets when he passed out in front of the TV.

"You haven't told her anything," a voice complained.

Cassie wanted to groan. She knew that voice. Nate was at her house, and from the looks of it, he possibly spent the night. They were really taking this joke too far.

"I told her as much as she needed to know," John replied gruffly.

"She needed to know more. She *needs* to know more,"

Nate corrected.

"I didn't know she was planning to take the exam. I would have told her *no*," John added, defensively. It was strange to hear him up so early without being angry.

"Well, she'll be moving in with me today. We already got a room ready for her. My mother will be by to collect her later," Nate told John. Cassie had never heard anyone talk so directly to her uncle before, especially no one her age.

"You can't just waltz in here and take her from me," John replied. Cassie could picture his face, hearing the words that were almost tipped with ice.

"I can, and you know it. If you wanted to be in charge, you should have gotten married like everyone else. You'd have complete control of your totem if you had." Nate seemed to not notice how deadly John's voice had become, or maybe he didn't care. Cassie guessed it was the latter.

John growled, and Cassie jumped, knocking into the picture on the wall. She caught it as it slid off the nail holding it. It was a good catch, but didn't count. The guys both stopped talking.

"Cassie," John called to her.

She was caught. She hated her uncle's super hearing.

Cassie walked around the corner into the kitchen. Nate was lounging at the table with an empty plate in front of him. He was still wearing the clothes from the night before. Nate ran his hands through his hair, patting it down a bit from where it was sticking out. Cassie's intuition over who slept on the couch seemed to be confirmed, but she didn't really want to know.

"The Bays would like it if you'd move in with them for the remainder of the school year," John stated, trying to hide his anger. He said it like it was an invitation, though she had heard otherwise.

"No thanks," Cassie replied, going over the stove to see if there was any food left. John was a jerk most of the time, but he was a great cook and always made large quantities.

Nate jumped up and followed right behind Cassie. She ignored him.

"It wasn't a question," Nate told her. She didn't even turn around.

Cassie opened the top of the frying pan. The eggs and hash browns left over were still warm.

"Umm, yeah. I live in a free country. Where I live is my choice, and I choose to stay here." Cassie walked past Nate without looking at him. She grabbed a plate from the cupboard next to where John stood, leaning against the counter, smirking at Nate.

"My mother will be by later to pick you up and make sure you have everything to apprentice with her," Nate said as he shifted to stand next to Cassie while she dished out her food.

"I haven't made my choice yet, but I wasn't even considering your mother. I was thinking I'd probably do best to apprentice with my aunt if I can talk the coven into it. She's technically blood, but since she's my aunt, I'm half different. I thought that argument might work," Cassie added, her plate full of food as she made her way to the table. Nate moved to block her way, and Cassie just stepped around him. She didn't think the argument would work, but she didn't need to tell Nate that.

"It isn't a choice. You're my mate and will do what I say." Nate huffed, putting his hands on his hips and looking like he was about to throw a temper tantrum like a two-year-old.

Cassie sat down at the table and started to eat her food. Nate was behaving like a spoiled child that wasn't getting his way. She had to try hard to not stoop to his level and argue back, and it was well worth it. Her calm disposition was making him even madder. His face began to turn red as he tried to sputter out some words.

"I have no plans to go anywhere with you," Cassie replied, interrupting him. She picked up more hash browns on her fork and looked at them, not at Nate. "I'm not your mate, and you're a bit crazy."

Cassie easily could have added 'hot' to her description of him, even after sleeping in his clothes, but she wasn't going to admit that. Cute as he was, last night was full of crazy. She wasn't going to play that game.

Nate threw his arms in the air in frustration.

"Ugh! This is all your fault for not telling her anything." Nate pointed his finger at John. "I will be back with my mother and *father* later to collect her. We will see if she can tell the alpha *no*."

Nate walked out the back door, slamming it behind him.

John chuckled from the window above the sink as he watched Nate storm away.

"Man, I wish I had met your father. He had to have been one powerful night human for you to be able to stand up to all that energy." John grabbed a plate and filled it with the last of the food, his second breakfast.

"Night human?" Cassie asked.

It wasn't often John was in such a good mood so early. It was even odder that he was in a good mood because she had been a brat. She couldn't help it; Nate pushed her buttons by ordering her around.

"Nate said he told you about us last night, and that you didn't believe him," John replied, digging into his food.

"Not you, too," Cassie complained under her breath, still waiting for John to growl at her. Instead, he just laughed. Something had put him in a really great mood.

"Yes. Me, too, and yes to everyone else in town. You wanted to be part of this, so suck it up and believe in it," John replied. His plate was half empty. He could inhale food like it was nothing. Cassie wasn't even certain he had chewed it.

"And all that *mate* crap?" Cassie asked. Would John really make her live with Nate and marry him at such a young age?

"Oh, that stuff is true, also," John answered, taking a

swig of milk that emptied one of the two full cups he had in front of him.

"And the *living with him* part?" Cassie wrinkled her nose at that idea. John shrugged.

She really didn't want to apprentice with Mrs. Bay. She didn't do anything fun for the coven. She was more of a secretary than anything, and Cassie didn't want to do that for the rest of her life. The town was boring enough without such a dead-end career. Cassie wanted to be out in the world. Traveling, seeing sights, helping others, just like Aunt Maria.

"When will Aunt Maria be back?" Cassie asked. Aunt Maria was the key. She would know how to play the system and get Cassie to apprentice with her. Cassie knew it. Aunt Maria had never let her down.

His smile faded a bit. "I don't know."

She took another bite of her eggs. Uncle John's food was all gone, but he didn't move to stand up from the table. Her head was bursting with questions. It had been a long while since John had been this happy; Cassie kind of wanted to try pressing her luck and getting all the answers she needed. She looked at him while she chewed and thought about which question to ask next. First, she had to know what the current situation truly was.

"Will Nate really be back later?" Cassie asked. She was a bit worried. Nate made it sound like John wouldn't be able to help her.

"Unfortunately," he replied, stacking his cups on his plate. "Why'd you go and have to do that exam? The Bays have been looking for a way to have you for years. I did just about everything I could to keep you from them. I even had the coven ban you from everything until you passed your exam."

"You did that to me?" Cassie asked in disbelief. She felt very lost her whole life, like she belonged nowhere, and to find out John did it was a low blow.

"Cas," John said, his hand grabbing her arm quicker than humanly possible as she tried to stand and leave the table.

Cassie glared at him and thought of using a spell on him. She knew at least ten that would hurt him temporarily, and she was very tempted to use one, but the look in his eyes made her stop.

"Cassie, we need to talk," John told her, letting go of her arm. He stood, and she stared in shock at him. He was never that reserved, and he was anything but nice to her not just most of the time, rather *all* of the time in the fall.

Following her uncle to the living room, she watched him open the coffee table in the middle of the room and pull out a box below all the family photo books. Handing Cassie the box, he went to his seat in his recliner and sat on the edge as he watched her. She continued to stare at him, and he motioned for her to open the box.

Slowly, she lifted the lid off the box and found a knitted baby blanket inside of it. There was a photograph with it, but nothing more. Cassie looked at the picture of a young couple with a baby. The baby was wrapped in the blanket Cassie now held. She felt the edges of the blanket in her fingers and closed her eyes. Turning it over in her hands, she rubbed the stitching, then opened her eyes to look at it.

Cassandra Aisling

Cassie already knew that was her name, but to see it on the blanket confirmed her suspicions about the picture. She had never seen her parents before. It should have been a shock, but it wasn't. It was the mother and father she had never met and would never meet. They were dead. It didn't hurt badly when she learned that before the exam, but seeing the two young faces in the picture made her finally feel it.

Her mother looked so much like her aunt it was unbelievable—they could have been twins. Her dark, almost black, hair hung long to frame her face and chocolate brown eyes. Cassie always wished to have those same eyes to fit in better with her family instead of the more honey brown color she had, but now she saw it. Her father was as fair as her mother was not. He was taller than her by over a head, with light sandy blond hair and crystal blue eyes. The magical color reminded her of the sky and the witches she had met over the summer. They all had blue eyes like that.

"Over sixteen years ago I got a call from your mother. She needed my help and couldn't come to me. She gave me an address on the other side of town. There, I found a man waiting for me. He handed me a baby that wasn't even a week old, and that photo. He kissed you, said some words to you in another language, and then left. I never saw or heard from them again. I hoped that they would come back some day. I knew that if my sister was around, she would do anything to get back to you. It wasn't like Gabbi to leave family. I know she would have never left you unless there was a reason. I was hoping one day I would learn what it was."

John watched Cassie, waiting for a reaction, but she didn't reply.

"As you grew up, I got the feeling you were a bit different than everyone else. You seemed to come into your witch powers much younger than most, and when you began to tell me stuff about people that I knew you shouldn't know, I tried to keep you a secret. It didn't work. I knew that as soon as the coven found out about you, they would use you, so I did the only thing I thought would keep you safe. I told them that your father wasn't from here and that you might not be part of the skinwalker line."

"Skinwalker?"

"You've been told that there are two types of humans—night and day—correct?"

Cassie nodded.

"The night humans that live here are called skinwalkers. Our family line is from the skinwalkers, which, by default, makes you one."

"Makes me a blood-drinking monster?" Cassie had never

craved anything in her life beyond chocolate, and she was pretty sure they didn't keep blood around the house to drink either.

John laughed. "You had to pick up on that part. No, you are not a blood-drinking monster. For most of us, the males inherit the gene to be a skinwalker, and the females to be a witch."

"So you're a blood-drinking monster?" Cassie was only half teasing as she smiled at her uncle. It had been years since he had been nice to her for so long.

"Blood-drinking monster? I guess you could describe us that way, but that brings to mind more of a horror movie. I'm a skinwalker, as my father was and his father before him. Your mother and aunt are witches, just like you and your grandmother. Your father showed up when he gave you to me, and I could smell he was a night human, but I couldn't come up with any other reason to keep you from the coven," John explained.

"So you knew my father, then?" Cassie asked tentatively.

"No. I had never seen him before that day, or again. It's just that to be here in town, he had to be one of us. Most night humans are territorial. That's why we never really have outsiders come to town. Anyone here has to be of the skinwalker bloodline."

"And how do you know that?"

"There are wards around our territory and the scent keeps everyone out that shouldn't be here. Did you ever wonder why I never let you leave town? If you were to accidentally go into another night human territory, it would mean negotiations to get you back if they found you," John explained. He was still watching Cassie to gauge her reactions to all of it.

"But we live in a free country. We can travel and go where we want," Cassie replied.

It sounded ridiculous the night before, but coming from John, she knew there was no joke. He didn't know how to joke.

"You? Yes, you are a day human. Me? No, I'm a night human. We have to keep apart. Night humans don't mix. Rather, they never used to mix. That's changing, too, but it's a tale for another day. For now, you need to know the basics." John watched Cassie. She didn't go running from the room, so that was a start.

Cassie continued to finger the blanket. It felt real and for some strange reason, it felt like home. She imagined the sheep that was shorn for the wool, and how it was woven into the blanket. She could almost see her mother doing it from beginning to end. That was more than strange. Her mother was a city person and had never lived on a farm, yet she enjoyed making the blanket.

"What are the basics?" Cassie asked tentatively, breaking the connection she had with the blanket and the images it was inducing in her.

"We live by the rule of one couple. The leader of the skinwalkers is the alpha and the leader of the coven. Most of the time, the leader is married to the alpha."

"But Mrs. Bay doesn't lead the coven," Cassie pointed out.

"I said most of the time. I kind of screwed things up a bit. I was supposed to marry Holly Carsen and take over when Mikel stepped down. I chose not to marry her, so currently she's the high priestess while Mikel is still the alpha."

"Alpha, like werewolf stories alpha?" Cassie made the only connection she could.

John shook his head with faked disgust. "Really? You had to go there?"

Cassie smiled. It was fun to have her old uncle back.

"Fine. We'll go with that. Anyone who is part of the clan must follow the alpha's orders. It isn't a choice. In a couple hours, when Nate brings his father with to collect you, I'll have to hand you over to them. Nate's father is our current alpha, and I am not," John explained.

"Wait. You're going to make me move away?" Cassie asked in disbelief. The Uncle John she was now talking to was so kind, she thought maybe he was actually the one she wanted to live with.

"I don't want you to go anywhere. That's why I fought the coven all the time about you. I wanted to protect you, but there's nothing I can do now. In two weeks you'll join the coven, and you are theirs to use just like they use Maria. You will have no choice but to do what they want." Standing, John motioned for Cassie to follow.

"But what if I don't want to go?"

John smiled. "I don't know if they've ever run across someone that won't do what they want. But it won't matter. You stand no chance against three skinwalkers and a witch. You will be forced to do their bidding."

Three? Nate, his father, and who else is coming with them? Cassie looked up at her uncle. And John. He nodded as the realization set in. She had taken him for granted all the years, but he probably was the only one keeping her safe.

"Do you remember when you were a kid, and Maria took you camping?" John led her into the kitchen.

Of course Cassie remembered. It was a disaster. They couldn't get the tent pitched, and the potion supplies got rained on so they couldn't use them for magic. It didn't just rain but poured all day and night. Yes, that was a trip Cassie would never forget.

"Maria said there was some place you guys found that could be an emergency spot," John continued as he opened the cupboards and began to pull out food.

Cassie wanted to ask what was going on but didn't even know where to begin.

"Pack as little as you can, make sure to take those stinky outdoor clothes you have in the back of your closet. Walk through streams and keep your scent hidden. Go to that place and stay there until Maria returns. I can't refuse the alpha as I am a skinwalker, but Maria is almost as strong as you.

Without being married into the coven, she can make her own choices. She will help you." John grabbed a brown paper bag and packed up all the food he had taken out.

"Are you telling me to run away?" Cassie asked in disbelief. She knew exactly the clothes John was talking about. She had them in the back of her closet and kept them there because he had said they stunk. She figured if she needed to get away some day, they were the only clothes she had that didn't smell like her, and since her uncle seemed to be part bloodhound that would be needed.

"I can't ask you to do that. In fact, as soon as they get here I'll have to help them. It is better if I don't know anything," John replied.

"But you haven't even told me what a skinwalker is," Cassie added as John put the bag of food in her hands.

"That lesson will have to wait. Now you need to leave, and I need to call my little sister," John pushed Cassie toward the stairway.

"But ..." Cassie wanted to resist more, but he had already pushed her up one stair and was gone from behind her when she turned around.

Cassie had ridden her uncle's moped as far as she thought was safe before hopping off. Yes, her big, burly uncle rode a moped. It was a sight to see, and she was a little sad to just leave it in the parking lot at the park. She got the understanding from her uncle this needed to be a very covert operation.

Cassie walked into the park and quickly found the stream leading to the lake she spent many hours at in the summer. She began walking down the stream, doing her best to ignore the freezing water as it seeped into her shoes.

The trees above waved in the wind as it began to pick up. The breeze was cool, but it would be close to freezing once the sun was down. The hike was going to take a few hours, and she had to backtrack around town to head the opposite direction of where she parked her uncle's moped. She never did have a lot of time to spend outside with all the time she had spent learning, but she knew enough about how to cover her trail. She had been out with her aunt on several occasions and was beginning to think it might have been training all along for this very day.

Cassie stepped out of the stream and began her walk up the hill. She'd like it better on the way down, but then she would be in another river.

It took longer than Cassie had wanted, but since she stopped every thirty minutes to cast a covering spell, she should have expected that much. The run-down cabin was hidden ahead, but with her keen sense of the trees around her, she knew exactly where it was.

She circled around the cabin. There was no magic she could feel. Cautiously, she approached the front door. It creaked loudly as it opened. Cassie stood on the porch, careful not to step on the places where the wood was rotting. The cabin was as musty and dusty-smelling as the last time they were there five years ago. In fact, it didn't look like much had changed.

Cassie set her backpack down inside the door. Then she emptied her pockets of the plants she'd collected on her five-hour walk. She'd need to get more to make potions, but the variety was limited in the woods surrounding town. That's why even the school had their own garden.

The old cabin had seen better days, but nothing really mattered. It would be a roof over her head, and once she got the protection spells set up around it, she would be able to live okay in it for a few days. Cassie began crushing the plants with her fingers. She didn't dare bring any of her witchling supplies with her in case they could track her by them. Something about how much John was afraid made her be cautious. Cassie gagged on the taste of the yellowcress as she chewed it up. She much rather have water from the sink to mix it with, but she didn't want to try anything in the cabin until she was sure no one would hear, see, or smell her.

The spell was easy to complete, but Cassie was far from being able to relax and eat whatever John had packed for her. She needed to collect firewood before it became too dark, and fill the bucket inside with the water from the pump just down the steps from the back door.

When the old cabin had been warmed, and after she had collected the water and the wood, Cassie finally opened the bag. John had packed enough canned food to last her days. Cassie was beyond caring what she ate as she took the top can and opened it.

"Chicken noodle soup it is," Cassie said to the empty room as she poured it into the cast-iron pan. She would have to hold it over the fire to heat it up.

The fire continued to burn as the sun set, and Cassie sat and ate her food. It was late, and she was exhausted. Unrolling her lightweight, but super-warm sleeping bag, Cassie was set for her first night away from home alone. Never once had she been alone like this. She had left the town several times while growing up, but always with Maria. She never found it strange that John always stayed behind, but now his explanation made more sense.

Cassie settled into her sleeping bag as close as she could get to the fire but where she still felt safe. It, more than likely, would go out sometime during the night, but that was fine. She would collect more wood in the morning.

The night was mostly silent except for the wind that easily made it through the cracks of the walls in the dilapidated cabin. The place was better than nothing, but still not completely warm. The fire was already slowly dying as Cassie dozed off to sleep. It didn't take long, as exhausted as she was.

Warm and fuzzy inside her bag, Cassie didn't notice the noise outside until she heard it a second time. The first time she thought it was part of her dream. It wasn't. Something outside was making a low-pitched groaning noise. Cassie sat up more quickly than she ever knew she could and was out of her restrictive bag almost as fast. She hurried over to her backpack and grabbed the only spell she had on hand. Cassie whispered the words and touched the goo to her forehead. She hoped her impromptu invisibility spell would be enough to keep her hidden.

The only place that didn't have cracks was right next to the window that faced the porch. Cassie crawled over and hid there. She had a great view of outside, but from the sounds of it, she kind of got the feeling she didn't exactly want to see what was making the awful noise.

Cassie held her breath as the sound came closer. She continued whispering the words; the spell had to work.

About ten feet from the cabin, a creature came slinking into view. It had large arms that stretched down to its knees, which were bent backward like an animal's. Its head wasn't human, though it was walking upright, and it was covered with patches of fur. It was a scary sight to see as it walked, but when it turned its eyes to Cassie, and their piercing red glowed in the dark, Cassie couldn't help but suck in a breath. It was like the creature was looking straight at her. Her spell didn't work, and she was screwed.

Cassie froze in place at the sight of the animal. Its mouth opened into a smile to show off its large razor teeth dripping with saliva and something else darker in color. The moonlight made it possible to see but still not clear. If she didn't know about the night human world, Cassie would have thought she was still dreaming. Now she was stuck in a broken-down cabin with a monster looking at her like she was going to be supper. Without a doubt, this was one of those night humans that feasted on humans. She regretted not asking more questions of John.

There weren't many options. She could try to run from the back door, but Cassie had a feeling that the creature could see better, and probably run faster, in the evening light than she could. She could stay inside and hope that it didn't have the dexterity to open the door. Then again, it could probably just push a hole in the decrepit walls. Her limited supplies and spells could be used to fight back, but it seemed that the invisibility spell didn't work, so would anything else? Cassie now wished her uncle was the hunting type—he could have given her a gun to run away with. This wasn't safe.

The creature turned and stared at Cassie. Slowly, it took a step forward. Its mouth hung open as it groaned, and its knees creaked. Cassie's heart began to beat faster. She was out of options. Nothing seemed like it was going to work. The monster's smile grew, and it took another slow step, as if he heard her heart beating out of her chest. She was going to die of a heart attack before anything else. The creature moved to walk forward again, but froze in his place. It tilted its head, paused a second time, and then moved faster than Cassie thought it could. It was gone in the blink of an eye and another flash of white streaked through the woods in the direction the monster left. Cassie frantically looked out the window. Where did the monster go?

CHAPTER 5

Cassie slept very little as she stayed in her spot by the window. The monster never came back, but Cassie had the feeling she wasn't alone. Someone was out there. She had to hope it was John that had scared that thing away, but she wasn't sure. John didn't know where the cabin was. Maybe he had got ahold of Maria, and she told him where to find Cassie. Either way, she had stayed safe by some miracle.

When the sun was finally up, Cassie felt safe enough to drift off to a solid sleep. It was going to be a long wait for her aunt if she stayed awake all night because there were monsters in the woods. She needed her rest, and had to use the safety of the sun to sleep and hope the monsters were sleeping, too. Unfortunately, Nate seemed to be right about that one. Things that went bump in the night were certainly outside the cabin last night. In fact, Cassie wasn't sure she could even imagine something that grotesque and scary if she had been asked to.

By lunch time, Cassie was rested enough to get up. The fire was completely extinguished since she hadn't moved all night, and her stomach was growling for sustenance. She would have to find wood before she'd get to eat anything since she needed the fire to cook everything John had sent with her.

It was easy to get into doing chores around the cabin. She had to collect wood, herbs, plants, and water. She had to reset her spell and hopefully do it better this time. It would have been nice to have a cell phone and call her uncle to ask questions, but Modern Survival 101 told her not to bring it with her. She could still be tracked by it.

As evening approached, Cassie let the fire burn down. Maybe it was the smoke that drew in the monster. She might have thought Nate was crazy the night before, but she felt she should have known better. If there were real witches, why wouldn't there be real monsters as well? The spell had been doubled, but Cassie still worried. She had no way to fight back if anything did happen, and after how quickly the gigantic thing disappeared, she had no chance to run away from it either.

The last of the sun's rays hid behind the horizon, and she was alone. The sky darkened quickly to black, and the clouds let the almost-full moon illuminate the woods around the cabin. Cassie huddled in her blanket by the window and waited.

The wind howled outside the cabin and began to lull Cassie to sleep. She was almost to dreamland when she heard it. This time, it wasn't a moan. This time, there were words. Someone was outside the cabin.

Cassie sat up as quietly as she could to get a better view outside the window. She couldn't see anyone, but she was sure she heard them. Standing just as quietly, she made her way to the window on the other side of the door. From there she could barely make out several people outside the range of her spell. One was talking to the rest of the group and pointing toward the cabin.

The group of people began to spread out as they walked toward the cabin. Running from a monster was one thing, now there were at least a dozen or more people walking her way. Cassie scooted under the window and back to the other side of the door. She had it barred and blockaded shut, but this was just getting to be too much. Her secret cabin didn't seem to be so much of a secret.

The people in the woods continued to move near. When they passed the tree line, Cassie would get a better view with the bright moonlight. She waited. Were they friends or foes?

Was the coven coming to collect her and force her to move in with Nate? She didn't know what sort of power the alpha had, but her uncle was afraid. That was enough to tell her to stay hidden.

The first person walked forward, and Cassie had to hold in her gasp of surprise. The younger man, whom she didn't recognize, quickly went from looking like a normal person to the same creature that had been in the woods the night before: elongated arms, backward knees, and a larger than normal head with fangs that would make anyone have a heart attack. *Not friendly.* These were bad people.

Cassie desperately looked around the cabin for someplace to hide. She wasn't going to take any chances sitting in the room this time. Her savior didn't seem to be anywhere nearby, and even so, could the person actually scare off a dozen of these?

There were cupboards that lined the wall by the old tin sink. It was possible that Cassie could fit in them. But would that really be a hiding place? Any normal person would check those if they were searching the cabin. She needed a better, less obvious, spot. She glanced around quickly. There was a sort of couch and a dresser. Again, not the best places to hide. Beyond that, there was a broken table and chairs that even a small animal couldn't hide behind. This wasn't good. Cassie already cast an invisibility spell, but that wouldn't matter either. These creatures seemed more animal than human. It was possible that they didn't even use sight to find her to begin with.

Cassie glanced back outside. One of the smaller monsters was approaching the house. This one was golden in color and didn't blend into the darkness around it. It's almost feline-like face peered at the door before the monster bent back and sat down, squatting right outside the doorway, with its back to the entrance. Cassie was trapped inside.

Was this the monster that had scared the others away the night before? She had seen flashes of white in the trees all night, but she didn't know what it was. The golden monster didn't even look back at the house; it just sat and stared ahead at all the weird monsters passing by.

As they neared the house, not a single monster stepped closer. This had to be her protector. Cassie had to hope that; otherwise, this was the monster that was strong enough to claim Cassie as its own personal supper.

Cassie peered from the window down at the monster. It had now curled up at the doorway like a cat. The other monsters paid no attention to the cat monster at the door, but they all each stopped near the house to give a good sniff before walking away.

Something was strange with the creatures. For one, not a single one was the same. Cassie got a better look as they passed and each had their own distinct face markings. Some appeared cat-like; others more like wolves or dogs. A couple looked like a bear if you squinted, and one even looked like a snake, slithering tongue and all. But they all appeared very animalistic. Was that what a skinwalker was? Closer inspection now showed her that none of them looked like the red-eyed one she had seen the night before.

Cassie kept standing at the window as she watched. The back of the house had a small escape door, but none of those monsters were even close to fitting through. She was safe that way. The only worry now was the golden cat at the front of the house, blocking the door. It wasn't like Cassie was going to go for a midnight stroll, but it was a bit nerve-wracking to sleep with that thing outside the cabin.

The fire was low, and the room was growing cooler as the night air seeped into the cabin. Cassie slid her blanket around her as best she could. She couldn't bundle into it like the night before because then she wouldn't be able to make a run for it, but she also was freezing. Cassie sat and let the blanket cover her legs also. From her position, she saw out the doorway if the cat monster stood, but she couldn't see it as it napped. It was going to be a long night.

Without much to do but sit and listen to her heart beat uncontrollably, Cassie couldn't help as her eyes began to close on their own. She tried her best to stay awake, but she just wasn't a night person. After being up the night before, she was exhausted. Something about the cat monster made her feel safe, like it was protecting her. Cassie wanted her fear to keep her awake, but it was slowly going away as she grew heavier and heavier in her warm blanket. When her eyes finally won and closed down, Cassie nodded off into a dreamless sleep.

Cassie woke with a start the next morning. She didn't know when she fell asleep, but it didn't take long to remember the night before. The place had been surrounded by monsters. Cassie peered out the window from her spot on the floor. She didn't know what happened to the monsters during the day, and would have remembered anything like that if she had come across it in town. There was nothing, and the woods were back to normal. Even the birds were happily chirping in the cold morning air.

She stood slowly. This was getting weirder and more dangerous. Part of her wanted to return to her uncle, but she shouldn't. He had sent her out into the woods for a reason. He seemed scared for her. He would have contacted Aunt Maria right away. Cassie had to hold onto hope that Maria was already arriving home and would be out to collect Cassie before nighttime. She was unsure how another night in the woods would go otherwise.

The morning woods were beautiful as the sun peeked from between the branches of the high trees. Animals scurried around. A chipmunk chased another chipmunk, and a squirrel collected leaves. It was fall, and everything seemed to be readying for winter in the woods. Everything except the monsters. Cassie looked down where the cat monster had been and gasped in surprise. There was no longer a monster, but a person lying naked in her doorway in the cold. And she knew who that person was.

Whitney accepted the blanket as soon as Cassie put it around her shoulders.

"That's the part I'll never get used to." Whitney was bubbly and talked like she was well-rested, like hadn't spent a large part of her night transformed into a half-animal monster.

Cassie stared at her talking best friend before remembering she was completely naked and needed some clothing. Going over to her bag, she pulled out a sweatshirt and sweatpants. Whitney was far too tall to really fit in anything of Cassie's, but it was at least something.

"Used to?" Cassie finally asked.

"Yeah, changing back naked. I mean, the whole changing into a night human thing is kind of common around here, but they leave out the naked part. Can you imagine your first change when you wake up the next morning completely nude on the neighbor's lawn because you aren't used to your totem and go to the wrong house? Completely mortifying," Whitney talked away as she put the clothes on.

"You're one of them?" Cassie asked though in reality she didn't need to.

There was only one thing lying at her door last night, and it happened to be Whitney in the morning. Unless Whitney did some magic trick to trade places with the furry monster, it had to be her.

"No, I just like to take a naked jog in the woods early in the morning instead of going to school. It really wakes you up in this chilly weather, and the best part is you don't have to change out of sweaty clothes when you get home because you don't have any on," Whitney replied, grinning at Cassie. "Oh yeah, and I was a bit winded and thought this cabin looked like a nice place to take a nap in the buff."

Cassie's mouth hung open. Two sleepless nights and her best friend showed up like nothing strange happened; she wasn't prepared for joking or sarcasm. Whitney looked up from pulling the blanket back around herself. As she stepped forward, and Cassie couldn't help but take a step back. Her best friend was a monster at night; a very large, scary monster.

"Shoot," Whitney finally said. "Everyone thought it would be best if I was the one to check on you, but I didn't mean to scare you."

Cassie stared hard at her friend. There was nothing on her that would indicate that anything was different, beyond her nudity. All the long hair and the strange, cat-like face were gone. She looked a little disheveled, but Cassie had spent the night more than once at her house. Whitney didn't look any different than at any of those times.

"I'm going to sit down," Whitney told Cassie before slowly moving toward her again. Cassie flinched but stayed in place as Whitney sat on the old couch.

"You might want to sit. I think we have a bit to talk about," Whitney told Cassie, holding her hands up in surrender to show she had nothing in them.

Cassie didn't know what to do. Whitney was her best friend, but it was all a bit overwhelming. How did Cassie not know her friend turned into a monster at night? She missed that even after being friends for years.

Whitney patted the old couch and dust flew into the air, making her sneeze. Cassie laughed as she backed up. No one in their right mind would pat that old thing. Whitney was lucky she didn't just punch her hand through it.

"I think the floor is safer," Cassie replied, sitting down on the hardwood floor.

Whitney glanced back at the couch beneath her. She must have realized it also as she slid to the floor in front of Cassie.

"I'm sorry if I scared you last night, or this morning, or both," Whitney told her, concern lacing her voice.

"You weren't really the scary one. That was the one the night before," Cassie replied. Whitney was scary, but it was true that she wasn't as scary.

"The night before? We didn't come out here until last night," Whitney replied. "Shoot, where'd I leave my phone. I'll have to call Than about that." Whitney patted her loaned sweatshirt before laughing. "I suppose that will have to wait."

"Call Nate?"

"Well, he isn't in charge yet, but since he's next in line, we kind of have to report to him," Whitney explained.

"In charge? Report?"

Whitney stared at Cassie. "They said they had explained this all to you."

"They?" Cassie was still confused.

"Than and your uncle. They said that they told you everything before you ran away. John had no clue where you went," Whitney added, winking at Cassie.

John might not have known the exact location, but he did have an idea of where she had gone. What side did that leave Whitney on? She was Cassie's best friend, but now she wasn't sure of what anything meant. John, who had always been mean to her, was trying to help her run away from Nate. And now Whitney, the person that was always open with her, had just been talking about calling Nate to turn her in.

"I'm not sure what they were supposed to explain, but I kind of didn't believe them or think about it until that monster showed up outside the cabin the other night," Cassie replied. Whitney flinched at the word *monster*.

"I don't know about that, but I assure you, I'll find out," Whitney replied solemnly.

"Before or after you take me back and force me to live with Nate?"

"You don't want to go?" Whitney was shocked. She bumped her knees to Cassie's knees as they sat facing each other.

"Umm, no. Why do you think I ran away?" Cassie

replied. No. She didn't want to live with Nate. She didn't want to date him either. She was over that crush, but he didn't seem to think so.

"I just thought that since you guys are mated and all that you'd want to move in their place until the ceremony," Whitney kept talking.

"I'm not *mated* to anyone," Cassie quickly pointed out.

"But your neck," Whitney said in reply. She was now the one confused. Cassie would have joked with her at this point, but she still wanted to get it through to Whitney what was really going on.

"Means nothing. I'm not mated, dated, or anything else with Nate. Why won't you believe me when I say that?"

"It's not that I don't believe you. It's just that no one has ever had the mark of another without being their mate. I figured with your crush on him, it was all he needed to make the bond and that you were more than willing to bind your life to his forever." Whitney shrugged.

"I'm so over that crush."

"Not according to your marking," Whitney answered.

Cassie huffed. Why didn't her own mind and words matter? Everyone seemed to think the invisible mark was enough to make her do something she didn't want to do. Without thinking, Cassie rubbed the mark on her neck. It was an invisible, annoying mark.

"Well, I'm not one of you guys. I don't turn all furry in the moonlight," Cassie pointed out.

"Of course not. You wouldn't have been made into Than's mate if you were. We always mate witch to skinwalker."

"And you? Aren't you a witch and skinwalker?" Cassie tried out the foreign word.

"I'm the oddity. Every now and then a female is born that can change forms. I'm not really a witch, hence, the reason I'm failing all our witch classes," Whitney explained with a *who cares* attitude.

"You're not a witch? Then how can you do magic?" Cassie had seen her friend do spells, even if she were really bad at it with results that were unwanted. She still did them.

"Technically, anyone can learn witch magic, but to be good at it, you have to have some witch blood in your genes. To be able to do what you can do, you have to have a pretty clear witch line, one that you can trace back centuries. Witches always mate with skinwalkers, and we never leave the clans to keep the witch line pure."

That wasn't a lesson Cassie had learned in school or she would have asked more questions. *Keep the line pure.*

"So they didn't really tell you anything?" Whitney was still staring at Cassie.

"They said stuff, but I was a bit more concerned with the fact that Nate planned to kidnap me, and my uncle could do nothing about it. You didn't happen to hear if my aunt is back in town?"

"Wait a second. Do you seriously not want to live with Than?"

It was if Cassie's words were finally sinking in for Whitney. Cassie stared at her friend. *Finally.*

"No. Why won't anyone listen to me? I don't want to live with Nate. I don't want to date Nate, let alone *mate* with him. And I don't want to be a part of all this scary crap. You should have seen the one the other night. It had red eyes. Like really red eyes." Cassie couldn't help but freak out. No one was listening to her, and life had just turned into a scene from a freaky horror movie.

"But that doesn't make any sense. If you don't want to be with Than, why did you get his marking?"

"I. Don't. Know." Cassie was exasperated. She loved her best friend, but it didn't seem like Whitney was on her side.

Whitney rubbed her forehead.

"They sent me out here because they said that you ran away because of all this night human stuff. They said it scared you, and you ran. But that wasn't why, was it?"

Whitney was finally getting the whole picture.

"I didn't believe them about the monster stuff," Cassie said. Whitney flinched again. It was definitely the word monster that got to her. "They told me about night humans. I really didn't believe them. I ran away because John told me that only Aunt Maria could help me. He said he couldn't keep me with him now. I don't want to live with Nate, and I really don't want to apprentice to his mother."

"They want you to apprentice with Mrs. Bay?" Even Whitney scrunched up her nose at that idea.

"Yeah. Please don't tell them I'm here," Cassie begged. Aunt Maria couldn't be far away.

"They already know you're here. Why do you think I was lying outside your door last night?"

Cassie dreaded having to find a new place to hide. Her shoes weren't completely dry yet.

"Will they be here soon to get me?" Cassie asked. She stood and began packing her stuff away in her hiking bag. "I've got to find somewhere else to wait out Aunt Maria returning."

"She's not coming back right now. She might not be back for weeks," Whitney said as she watched Cassie run around the small cabin.

"Weeks?" Cassie asked, almost dropping the can in her hand. She would have to hide out in the woods with the monster for weeks? John made it sound like Maria would only be days.

"They aren't letting her come back now until you join the coven. Everyone knows that she would stop it. Heck, she's the only one that has ever joined the coven without a mate. No one else knows how or will tell anyone how to join without a mate," Whitney explained, still watching Cassie carefully.

"Wait a second. I can't join the coven without getting married? What sort of twisted world is this? Why the heck did anyone let me take the exam if that was the requirement?" Cassie was more than a little upset. Not even Whitney stopped her when she went to do the exam.

Whitney looked guiltily at her bare feet. "Owen and I didn't think you'd pass it, and if you did, he planned to ask you out and save you from all the mate stuff."

Cassie's eyes bulged at the answer. She didn't know what hurt more: her friends thought she wouldn't pass, or that they planned to set her up with Owen to have to avoid telling her everything. It was the same old stuff she grew up with. Even her friends were in on the secret. And man, what a secret it was.

"Owen planned to step in as my mate but not explain it to me?" Cassie asked for clarification. "Just like Nate did?"

"Kind of," Whitney replied.

"Is everyone crazy?" Cassie began to throw her stuff back in her bag.

"You didn't grow up knowing all of this. It isn't really too crazy to us. I mean, come on. First off, no one has joined the coven as a teenager in years, beyond your aunt of course, and second off, think back to all those couples from high school that are still together. Didn't you say just weeks ago how strange our school must be because everyone is still with their high school sweethearts? Well, this is why. Most night humans mate for life."

It was strange that everyone seemed to stay together, and Cassie had wondered about it. But she didn't want to be part of it. She didn't want to be with Nate, and everyone told her they were already partners. How many more didn't want to be with who they first dated in high school? It didn't sound like fun or a world she wanted to join. Cassie had spent her whole life wanting to be in on the secret and join the coven, but she didn't exactly like the terms.

Cassie grabbed the last bit of her stuff and shoved it in her backpack.

"You really are going to keep hiding?" Whitney asked cautiously, moving to stand with her friend.

"Yes. I'll hide until Aunt Maria comes home, even if they try to keep her away," Cassie replied.

"But what about joining the coven?"

Yes, that had been a lifelong dream, but Cassie didn't want to think about that now. She needed to stay safe and away from any of the monsters. She wasn't marrying or mating anyone, especially not Nate.

"You really don't want to be with Than?" Whitney asked for the umpteenth time in ten minutes while standing to follow her to the doorway.

Cassie looked up at her friend, who was now blocking the door. If she truly was that night human monster she saw the night before, she didn't stand a chance of getting by.

"No. I don't want to be with Nate. I have no idea what mark you are all talking about, but I don't want to be with him. I don't want to be with anyone like that. I want my own life to make my own choices. I knew the coven expected some sort of control. I got that. I saw how they treated Aunt Maria. But I didn't expect that they would force you to marry someone," Cassie replied, hoping it would finally sink in.

Whitney walked over and stood in front of Cassie.

"What can I do to help you, then?"

"You believe me?" Cassie asked in shock, really expecting the argument to continue.

"Cas, I thought you were just playing coy with us about Than. The only way a mating mark can show up is if you willingly kissed him and your unconscious side decided that you were a good match. But if you don't want to be with him, I believe you."

"We did kiss." Cassie's shoulders slumped. It had been her fault all along. She had asked to take the exam. She went behind her uncle's back, and she kissed Nate back.

Whitney's eyes shot wide.

"You kissed him. You didn't tell me that. You're supposed to tell your best friend stuff like that," she squealed. "Was he as good as everyone says?"

"I didn't kiss him. He kissed me. Besides, it doesn't matter. We might have kissed, but I stopped it as soon as I realized what I was doing. I don't want to be with Nate. Not then and not now. I want to make my own choices on everything," Cassie complained.

Whitney wiggled her eyebrows.

"And fine. He's a good kisser," Cassie added for her best friend.

"I knew it," Whitney exclaimed like she had won some sort of bet.

"Are you really going to help me?" Cassie asked.

"Of course. You're my best friend. Why wouldn't I help you?" Whitney placed an arm around Cassie and guided her back to the blanket on the floor.

Cassie looked at her friend. She was one of them, but she was still Whitney.

"Check me out." Whitney looked directly into Cassie's eyes opening the connection between them to show her how honest she really was. "I promise that I'm on your side. We just need to plan before heading back to town," Whitney explained.

"I'm not heading back to be married off to Nate." Cassie tried to pull away, but Whitney's firm grip didn't let her go anywhere.

"I'm not going to let them force you to mate with Than. If you don't want to be with him, then you won't. It will be over my dead body before I let them."

"But if you return me to my uncle, he said even he can't stand up to them. He said he'll have to do what the alpha tells him." Cassie still didn't sit.

"Yes, he does. He's a full member of the pack. Well, even the youngsters have to do what the alpha says, but it doesn't quite work that way with me." Whitney shrugged. "I'm part of the pack, but the whole bow down to the leader thing works when there is intent to harm or take over. I can't be the alpha, so I'm not a threat. The alpha can't compel me to do anything because he won't threaten me physically since I'm a girl. I kind of don't have to do what they want."

Cassie stared hard at her friend. She was tempted to look into her thoughts and see more, but she didn't. Of anyone, Cassie trusted Whitney. She trusted Owen also, but he didn't seem to be around at the moment.

"Then what can we do?" Cassie asked, finally sitting beside her best friend.

"Well, first off we need to make a plan. We can't head back without one. Than is waiting for us. I told him I would take care of you and return when we are ready. I just never said when I would bring you back. He can wait a little longer."

Some of the weight was gone. Cassie had felt alone, but now she saw otherwise. Whitney was her friend, even if she turned into a scary monster at night.

"If you let me get a fire going and promise not to run away without me, we can sit here until sundown making plans," Whitney said as she stood cautiously. "If you don't want to be bonded to Than, then I won't let him do anything. He might be the next one in charge, but that doesn't mean he can tell us all what to do."

"Isn't that what it means to be in charge?" Cassie asked.

"You know what I mean. You can't force someone to like you, and the bond is all about liking someone. He can't force that on you, even if he somehow found a way to claim you. Let me warm this place up. You have to be freezing. Stay here."

She nodded. It wasn't like she could outrun her night human friend if she wanted to, but she didn't need to. Whitney seemed to finally understand where Cassie was coming from. It might be a lot to learn and was more than a bit confusing, but she was feeling better. Whitney would help her. That's what best friends were for.

CHAPTER 6

The cabin didn't take long to warm up since it was small. Whitney was right; Cassie was freezing, but it didn't seem to affect her friend at all. It was as if she had an invisible fur coat on. Cassie sat huddled in the blanket as the warmth seeped around her.

"What's it like?" she asked her friend about being a night human. "Do you drink blood?"

Whitney laughed. "Of course they told you that part. I would have run screaming to the hills, too, if that was what people told me a night human was. Geesh. Men are idiots."

Cassie laughed. Her toes were finally unfreezing under the blanket. It was good to have Whitney there. Even if she was part of all the crazy, she was still Whitney. That made things a tad bit more bearable.

"Are you still you when you become a monster?" Cassie had tons more questions.

Whitney smiled from her spot at the fire she was stoking.

"Yes, I drink blood on occasion. Yes, I'm still me. And no, it isn't all bad." Whitney gazed out the window. "When you grow up like this, it's different than what you are going through. It doesn't seem strange. Even being completely in your totem on the full moon doesn't seem strange. And before you ask, that's when I typically drink blood, and yes it's animal blood. You aren't given human blood until you have a mate and become a full member of the clan."

Whitney was at the fire, cooking. "Did he really give you ham and beans in a can?" Whitney asked while she stirred. "Where does he find food like this?"

That was John. He knew how to pack protein into any meal, and it didn't surprise Cassie in the least.

"So tell me more about this bonding thingy. How do I avoid it?" Cassie asked.

Whitney pulled one of the cans from the fire without a mit. Her hand sizzled a little, but she didn't seem to care in the least. She set the warm can in front of Cassie, then Whitney wiped her burned hand with her other hand and a bit of skin flaked off, but she still didn't to even notice. Reaching back into the fire, she grabbed the second can.

"The bond is really simple. He ingests some of your blood, and you take some of his." Whitney dug into her food.

"Gross, but okay. And what else?" Cassie gingerly ate the steaming hot beans.

"Nothing else," Whitney added between bites. "It's that simple. Blood for blood exchange."

"But how do you donate blood at a hospital then? Or help an injured person? People can accidentally swap blood. It might not happen often, but it can. I mean, aren't there blood-borne diseases all over the place? How come people aren't bonded to night humans all the time?"

Whitney laughed. "Well first off, does it seem like we get hurt often? How many days of school do you think I've ever missed in my life? What about Owen? We don't exactly go into hospitals for anything. And blood donation? Nope. We're not allowed to do that at all. Night human blood can be used to turn someone into a night human if done correctly. We are not running around giving our blood out. Even witches can't donate their blood."

Cassie hadn't thought of that. Whitney had said it was best to think of her kind of like a cross between a vampire and werewolf, but Cassie figured she was kidding.

"So you really drink blood, like human blood?" Cassie finally went back to the original question.

Whitney cringed.

"Yeah, it's kind of required," Whitney replied, trying to shrug it off.

"Required?"

"All night humans need day human blood to live. It's part of being a night human. Some breeds of night humans only need blood once a year; some need it once a day. There are even a few groups that prefer flesh over blood. They are the ones we try to keep an eye on."

Cassie took another bite of her food. Whitney had been answering her questions all afternoon, but it was still strange. Actually, it was all weird. Cassie had felt like she woke up in a horror movie ever since she fell asleep at the campfire.

"There isn't the possibility that this is all a dream?" She wanted it to be true. Whitney sadly shook her head. "Or maybe an elaborate joke?" Cassie was grasping at straws. The great big secret she wanted to know all her life was turning into a nightmare.

"You wanted in on this world, so let me be the first to say, welcome to the world of night humans." Whitney gave Cassie a small smile as she looked behind her at the window. "I'd love to stay and talk more, but I have a feeling you'd be a bit scared as soon as the moon hits the sky."

"Do you change every night?"

"On the full moon, we all change. That's part of being a skinwalker. We only change on the other moons if the alpha orders it," Whitney explained as she stood up and began to undress.

"Is it safe for me to be left alone here?" Cassie asked.

The image of the monster from the first night was still close in her mind. Somehow she knew that monster wasn't one she wanted to see again. Whitney was scary, but even before Cassie knew it was her, she could trust her.

Whitney stopped at the doorway as the sky darkened and the room's only glow came from behind Cassie at the fireplace.

"It won't be as scary tonight. It's the full moon. Things

are different at the full moon. We aren't monsters, but we become our actual totem animal." Whitney opened the door, and a cold blast of air slipped in, making Cassie squint at her friend as she left.

"Wait," Cassie stood up and followed her friend to the doorway, "what is your totem?"

Whitney stopped at the tree line, blending into the darkness.

"I'm not supposed to tell anyone, but what can they do? I'm a cat," she replied, holding a hand up to wave to her. "You'll be safer inside. Shut the door until I return."

Cassie shut the door as her best friend disappeared into the night. Had someone told her a week ago she'd be watching her best friend run naked alone into the woods, she would have thought they were crazy. Now she was doing just that.

She walked back to the roaring fire that was keeping the place warm. It was nice that Whitney was able to get her more than enough wood to last the night. Her super speed really came in handy. Cassie was eager to learn more about all of it. If Aunt Maria found a way out, they needed to get her home before they could force Cassie to leave. Too bad Maria had her whole life to know about it and plan a way out. Cassie had less than two weeks.

It wasn't long before Cassie heard scratching at the door. She went to the window first to peer out, and sure enough there wasn't a monster there like the night before, but a large cat, a tiger to be exact. The tiger looked up at the window like she could sense Cassie was staring at her. When the tiger scratched the door again, Cassie went to the door and opened it a crack. Was it even safe to let her friend in? When she was a monster the night before, Cassie hadn't even considered it, but the furry cat at the window seemed less scary than the monster.

Cassie shook her head. A full-grown tiger seemed less scary. What had she gotten herself into? The night human world was just getting weirder and weirder by the moment.

"When you said cat, I was imagining something more like a house cat," Cassie said to the large tiger that walked right into the room. The white, black, and orange stripes looked soft to touch, but Cassie had the feeling that petting her friend might be offensive.

The tiger huffed.

"Or maybe a bobcat," she suggested. Cassie wasn't expecting an animal that stood almost as tall as her on four legs, and she was on two.

The tiger tapped the door with her paw to indicate for her to shut it. She obliged, and without the draft, the heat from the fire began to warm the room again. Cassie sat back down and wrapped herself in her blanket. In a normal life, she would never be calm with a full grown tiger in the room. The cat was huge. Cassie had never seen tigers up-close beyond the zoo, but even then, this one had to be twice the size of a normal tiger.

"So you stay like this all night?" she asked.

Her friend nodded.

"This is strange. If this dream gets any stranger, I might not want to go back to reality," Cassie teased.

The tiger tilted her head, as if to question Cassie.

"Yeah, yeah, I know. This isn't a dream. But you do have to cut me some slack. It isn't every day I find out my best friend turned into a cat, and then moments later sit in a rundown cabin with her as she stares back at me through tiger eyes."

The cat almost smiled.

"And you understand everything I say," Cassie assumed. The tiger nodded.

"This is going to be a long night. You have much more explaining to do for me. One night you are a monster and the next a cute, furry kitty."

The tiger growled.

"Sorry. Ferociously cute kitty," Cassie corrected. Her

friend seemed to accept that description. "This whole night human world is confusing. I wish someone had let me in on the secret years ago."

Tiger Whitney walked closer to Cassie and sat down next to her. Cassie gazed into her bright blue eyes. The humanity behind them shone clearly. Even though she looked like a cat, Whitney was still inside the animal. The tiger nudged her head under Cassie's hand, surprising her.

"You want me to pet you?" she asked. The tiger picked up her head, and Cassie's hand went down from her head to her neck; the tiger bowed down and made Cassie pet her again.

Cassie laughed.

"Don't think being cute will get me to forgive you easily. You still owe me. You spent years not telling me anything about this. You should have told me. We're best friends. Friends don't keep secrets, at least not like this."

Tiger Whitney nodded.

Cassie continued to pet the head of her friend. The fur was much softer than she expected.

"What are we going to do?" Cassie finally began talking again when the silence began to get to be too much. "If they won't let Aunt Maria come home then my choice is bond to someone I don't want to be bonded to, or leave."

The tiger's head shot up at the words of leaving and nipped playfully at her hand.

"You know I can't stay here. If we don't find a way out of this, I can't stay. I don't want to be forced to be with someone, no matter what that magical mojo decided. I get to decide who I'm going to marry, bond with, or whatever. No one gets to make that choice for me. Right now I just want to go home and sleep in my own bed without having to worry that someone is going to come to my uncle's house and force me away. You wouldn't have believed how nice he was before I left. I'm completely telling the truth. Now I won't get time to just be with him in a good mood for a change."

The tiger peered at her as she spoke.

"This would be so much easier if I could mind read, or if you could speak. I mean, come on. You change into a fully grown tiger at night. Why can't you be a speaking tiger?"

The tiger snorted, and Cassie laughed. It was almost as if they were laughing together. Cassie missed those moments when Whitney was gone. There had been sleepovers, but there were times that Cassie needed a friend to give her strength when dealing with John. Whitney had missed lots of those moments over the year. Now she understood why. There was no way Whitney would be around to answer a phone on a full moon.

"Do you ever wish things were different?" Cassie asked the tiger, even though it could obviously not respond. "I do. I wish I knew my mother. I wish people would have talked more about her. I wish I had been included in this weird world rather than have it forced upon me. I wish I had a choice in all of this and could just be me. Why do I have to decide on everything right now? I'm just a kid. Why can't I be worried about a prom date like everyone else, instead of a guy I don't know forcing me to marry him? Why can't I just be normal?"

The tiger Whitney stood and rubbed her face against Cassie. The tiger licked her cheek with her rough tongue, and Cassie squealed. Cat affection at its best.

"I know, I've never been normal. I just wish I was. I mean, I don't even hate Nate all the time. You know how I told you he used to be friends with Owen and me? That's the Nate I still had a crush on last year, but that Nate is gone. The new one sucks big time, and there's no way I'm doing anything to bind my life to his. Who just claims a girl without explaining anything? We haven't even had a date, and I'm expected to essentially marry him. This night human world is way too messed up."

Cassie pulled the blanket around herself tighter. The more she talked; the more she felt the urgency for finding her aunt. She didn't want to leave her friends, and it wasn't fair that she was going to have to if she couldn't find a way out. This was the only life she knew. She didn't know where she could go. Aunt Maria was the key.

"I wish for once I had a normal life. A life where a guy actually felt like he had to be a gentleman and ask you out, not just kiss you and claim you. I want a prince, not an ass." Whitney had to agree on that; she was the one that had been saying it for years.

The tiger stood and came over to Cassie. She snorted before gently pushing the blanket off Cassie.

"Hey. We're not all blessed being that warm," Cassie grumbled at her friend. The tiger stood close enough Cassie could feel the heat radiating off the large creature. "No wonder you weren't cold. If I had a fur coat like that, I wouldn't be cold either."

The tiger stepped on the blanket as she wrapped herself around Cassie by lying down. Cassie was cautious at first with the large claws that she got a glimpse of as the tiger stretched, but once the warmth hit, she couldn't help it. It was more than warm and cozy to be wrapped in the tiger fur. Before long, Cassie let the warmth of the fire and her friend lull her to sleep. She laid her head on the nice furry pillow that was Whitney.

"I like this version much better than the red-eyed monster that came the other night." She yawned as the tiger's bright blue eyes stared intently at her. Cuddling into the soft fur, she patted the side of her friend a bit.

"I always wanted a kitty growing up," she joked as she closed her eyes.

Cassie woke the next morning to Whitney clanging cans together. Her back was to Cassie, and she was in the clothing Cassie had loaned her. She was standing at the fire, cooking away.

"Hey. Some of us were sleeping here," Cassie complained, pulling the blanket over her head.

"Yeah, well, some of us are in really big trouble for not bringing you back to town last night," Whitney retorted.

"But I thought you don't have to listen to them," Cassie replied, confused. Whitney made it seem like no big deal the day before.

"Do what they say? No. I don't have to like everyone else, but they can yell at me and make my life difficult if I don't do what they ask," Whitney answered, turning to Cassie from the fire and handing her another can of whatever John packed.

"So you're giving me back?" Cassie asked, saddened by her friend giving up.

"Giving you back? Hell no. Returning you to town with a plan. Would I ever do anything but cover my best friend's back?" Whitney winked at her.

"Then what's the plan?" Cassie asked, digging into her SpaghettiOs. Tomato pasta for breakfast wouldn't be missed. Cassie only hoped they would let her stay at home with her uncle when they went back.

"The library has a lot of books that only the coven can use. I think maybe we can use those books to find Maria," Whitney suggested. She stunk at spells, but Whitney was quite good at sneaking around.

"Why can't I just call her?" Cassie took another bite of the obnoxious breakfast. She would have to pretend she was eating her uncle's famous bacon omelets to get through another canned meal.

"They kept her phone from her. She didn't even get John's call. I told you; they're doing their best to keep her busy and away from here for the next week and a half. So we have to find a way to call her home," Whitney replied. "And I know exactly which books we need to look in. I saw one there the other day about traveling. I've seen my mother use locator calls before, too. I'm sure she got the spell from one of those books. We find the spell to get Maria, and we find your ticket to joining the clan without a bonding."

Cassie stared at her friend. She had a feeling it wasn't going to be that easy, but she was more than willing to try. She hated the idea of starting over. She didn't really have anywhere to go, but she would if they were still intent on forcing her into an arranged marriage.

"Let's get going soon. I could use a real meal," Whitney said as she stood and threw the empty can into the fire. Real food? She had already finished her canned breakfast before Cassie even got five bites of hers in.

"How do you eat that much and stay thin?" Cassie asked as she took a few more bites of her food. Whitney ate junk food all the time but never gained a single pound. She still turned eyes everywhere she went and ate almost as much as Owen at times.

"Night human metabolism."

Cassie shook her head and followed her friend who had already packed everything back outside and heading home. The trek back to town was easier since Whitney carried all the supplies and had a really good sense of direction. Cassie had wandered a bit to find the cabin, but Whitney was right on target getting them back. Cassie couldn't help but slow down as they made it to the edge of town. Was it really safe to go back?

"My car is over there." Whitney pointed to the parking lot of the grocery store.

Cassie half wanted to turn right around and go back into the woods. The only thing keeping her from doing so was the threat of the weird monster she saw the first night. She was more than certain now that Whitney had kept it at bay the past two nights. If she turned and ran from her friend, it was possible no one would be between her and the red-eyed monster.

"Come on," Whitney looped her arm in Cassie's, "I won't let them take you away."

Famous last words is what Cassie wanted to add, but her friend was being sincere. But even Whitney seemed to have to follow orders. Whitney threw Cassie's bag in the trunk while unlocking the car. Cassie paused a second time. Now she felt like someone was watching her. She glanced around the empty parking lot and saw no one. When she looked back to the woods, she saw a quick flash of white blur into the trees. That was enough for her to hurry up and hop in the car. She didn't need to see the monster again to know that it wasn't on the same side as her ... whatever side she was on.

Whitney had her phone in her hand and was scrolling through missed messages. Without calling anyone back, she closed her phone.

"Don't need to check in with the bosses?" Cassie asked.

"Nah. I told the alpha last night that I was with you and would bring you back today when he began to yell at me," Whitney replied.

"You had your cell phone all along," Cassie added, disappointed. She had spent a whole night with tiger Whitney having to entertain both her and herself. She could have at least been doing research online.

"No. It's been here the whole time. Changing doesn't exactly leave room to carry anything."

"Then how did you tell the alpha?" Cassie asked. There was much she needed to learn.

"You'll be a bit creeped out," Whitney warned.

"Try me."

"We can talk telepathically at night time. When you're part of the clan, you can communicate without words to the alpha," Whitney explained, watching Cassie for a reaction.

That didn't sound too creepy.

"So you what ... talk to each other all the time?" Cassie was looking for the creep factor.

"Not exactly." Whitney turned on the car and began the short drive back to Cassie's place. "More like mind reading, whenever the alpha wants."

"Wait a second; the alpha can look into your thoughts at any time?" Cassie asked, beginning to get worried.

"Yeah. Some man old enough to be my own father can look into my thoughts. Not a perk of being a skinwalker."

"And you didn't happen to mention that before you and I started to plan a way out of this?" Cassie was a little upset. All their planning was moot if the alpha could just look and see what they were doing.

"Give me more brains than that," Whitney complained as she reached for the radio to turn on. Cassie just stared at her friend. Whitney wasn't dumb at all. In fact, she was more the opposite. The only reason she was close to failing her witch classes was because it seemed like magic didn't like her. Everything Whitney did she had to try twice as hard as everyone else to get half the results.

"So how do we get around that one?"

"Not a problem. You seem to be a glitch in all that alpha control stuff. The alpha can see into all my memories, but not when you're in them. I found that out years ago, and he still doesn't know that I know. He's very tricky, and Than is learning from the best. But I know the truth, even if no one else does. You are hidden from the alpha, which gives us time and freedom to plan without anyone knowing, at least not through mind reading." Whitney grinned.

Whitney pulled her car to a sharp stop in John's driveway. There was already a car parked there, and Cassie half wanted to beg her friend to turn around and drive them out of town as quick as she could.

The front door to the house opened; it was too late to pretend they didn't make it home yet.

"I won't let them force you to do anything. I promise," Whitney told Cassie. "I got your back."

Cassie wasn't sure what that meant. So far all she knew was that Whitney could disobey the alpha, but that didn't mean she could stand up to him or Nate. What was going to stop them from physically making her leave with them?

Whitney got out of the car, walked around to Cassie's side, and opened the door.

"You're going to be fine," she tried to reassure her.

Cassie looked up at her friend bleakly. There was no use staying in the woods if John couldn't reach Maria. Whitney was right that they had to come back to find a way out of everything, but that didn't mean it wasn't terrifying.

"If he tries to force you to bond to him, I'll bond to you myself. So don't worry, you don't have to do anything you don't want to. I'll stand by you." Whitney held her pinky out for Cassie. "Bestie pinkie promise."

Cassie couldn't help but smile at that. Whitney was always making pinkie promises, and the best part was that she had yet to break a single one.

"Fine. But if I end up married with monster children, I will blame their Aunt Whitney for the rest of her life." Cassie took her friend's pinkie in her own. There wasn't much choice, and it was best to face it together.

Cassie walked up to her house with her waiting uncle in the doorway. He gave Whitney a grim smile, and she nodded back to him. Cassie held onto her best friend for support and to keep anchored. She was close to bolting again. She had to keep telling herself it was better to face the monsters she knew than the one she didn't.

John led the two girls into the living room. Nate was sitting, watching TV. He stood as soon as Cassie and Whitney entered. He looked to Whitney first, and then to Cassie.

"You didn't run into any trouble?" he asked, not divulging anything in particular.

"No," Whitney answered curtly.

"Good. We plan to have people run shifts around the house twenty-four seven," Nate continued. Whitney nodded in agreement.

"Shifts?" Cassie asked.

"You know the night human you saw the first night? That

wasn't one of ours," Whitney explained.

"What?" Cassie was getting a bit upset. What more was Whitney leaving out?

"I didn't want you to worry on the hike. It wasn't like they would attack in daylight anyway," Whitney added. "Now it isn't an issue. We're back, safe and sound."

"Obviously it is," Cassie replied. "Wait. Why would they be protecting my uncle?"

"Yeah," Whitney replied, both girls turning to Nate at the same time.

"He doesn't need protection," Nate replied, rolling his eyes at Whitney. Nate turned to Cassie, his expression serious. "You do since you want to stay here. John can take care of you while he's awake, but winter is coming, and he sleeps soundly at night."

That much was true, but Cassie had no clue how Nate knew that. She glanced at her friend who nodded in agreement with Nate.

"Okay, what am I missing now?" Cassie asked Whitney.

"Well, you know how we change into our totems at night?" Whitney began. "John isn't of the feline variety skinwalker."

Cassie looked over at her uncle who was back in his chair in front of the TV. She wasn't sure if he was listening to them or not. He didn't even turn to them as they talked about him.

"Then what is he?" Cassie asked, realizing John was back to sleep. At least that much seemed normal, even if the rest of her life was more than a bit messed up.

"What animal do you think he acts like?" Nate prompted.

Cassie shrugged. Her uncle slept through the winter months and had quite the temper. People often times described him …

"He's a bear?" Cassie guessed. Whitney nodded.

Everything about her childhood and being raised by John clicked into place. It all made much more sense now. The moody falls, and sleepy winters. Bulking up and endless meals all fall long to cold, slow, meager winters. Cassie had never seen a bear in the wild before, but everyone knew they hibernated for the winter. Cassie looked at Nate and Whitney, who were both waiting for her to do something.

"Do you think she's going to freak now?" Whitney asked Nate.

Nate smiled. "No. She's tougher than that."

Cassie shook her head. It all suddenly got a lot more real. She might have been able to pretend it was a dream, or the people around her were crazy. But they weren't. Cassie was now part of the world she wanted to be a part of since she was a kid. And it was nothing like she had expected to be.

CHAPTER 7

Returning to school was strange, and not just because Cassie had skipped a few days. It was weird because now instead of blending into the background, people actually looked at her. She had grown used to people ignoring her or even a few fearing her from her lack of control over looking into their memories in the past. Now people actually spoke to her. It was beyond bizarre. The amount of hello's she received on her way to her locker in the morning was enough to make her want to go back home.

At least she was going to get out of afternoon classes since she passed her exam. All she had to do was make it through the ten minutes of updates for the class and coven, and she would be free to be on her way. She already had plans to hit the library, and Whitney planned to go with her and skip her lessons. It turned out that Whitney had only kept taking the witch classes to be with Cassie once they became friends. As a skinwalker, she wasn't expected to take classes, so she was there by choice.

"And did you see how Corey Tegan almost bowed to you when you walked by?" Whitney whispered to Cassie as they sat in the auditorium, waiting for the teacher to talk. Whitney found Cassie's new celebrity status humorous, even more so that Cassie wasn't taking it well.

"That's not funny," Cassie complained. "Did you see how Jennifer looked ready to curse me on the spot?"

The guys had all taken to staring or being quite courteous to Cassie, but many of the girls were not as keen on her new status. It had only been half a day, but it was already apparent there was going to be something more happening. Most of the other witchlings-in-training had never liked Cassie, and her new-found status among the males of the school didn't help anything.

"You'll be fine. Since the mark Than put on you can only be seen by night humans, they're always slow to accept the news that someone is taken, especially by the next alpha," Whitney replied. Cassie had heard it all perhaps a dozen times since she complained to Whitney, but it didn't make it any better, nor was it a status she wanted to have. "When he makes it public, they can't do anything to you without being forced to leave the coven. They'll all get over it."

"Makes it public?" Cassie asked cautiously.

She had noticed Nate talking with the teacher for more than five minutes. How could she not? She noticed everywhere Nate was now. It was like she could feel him looking at her. Somehow she had developed Nate radar, and it was more than annoying. It was worse than when she had her crush last year.

Mrs. Anton cleared her throat, and the whole room began to settle down. Nate stood just to the side of the teacher, looking like he was bored, but Cassie knew otherwise. He was actually really anxious. He relaxed and leaned against the table, hiding his hand which was tapping out a rhythm. He always tapped his fingers when he was nervous. Cassie hated that she knew that much about him.

"The only upcoming event we have planned is still the ceremony for our own Cassie a week from Friday," Mrs. Anton began her list of updates. "You will all be expected to attend. It's not every day that I get to lead the ceremony, so I expect you all on your best behavior. For those of you going with your mothers to the retreat the week after, make sure you have all your work done prior to leaving. That only gives you two-and-a-half weeks to get caught up. Other than that, Nathaniel would like to address the room."

The room full of teenage girl witchlings grew excited

with chatter. Cassie tried to tune them out, but more than half of them were telling their neighbors about the one time they kissed him and how sure they were that they were going to be the next mate to the alpha. If she could, Cassie would have given that opportunity to any of the girls talking, but she still didn't know how. Cassie and Whitney couldn't get to the library soon enough to start researching.

"As some of you know, the seer predicted that I'd find a mate before leaving high school," Nate began, facing the crowd of female admirers.

He looked around the room, stopping his gaze on Cassie. All traces of nervousness instantly vanished.

"While I didn't think she was correct, it was a lesson I had to learn. I have indeed found my mate," Nate continued. The room filled with quiet excitement.

Cassie silently groaned. She didn't want this at all. First off, she didn't want to be his *mate*. Second, she was going to try to find a way around it as quick as she could. Nate making it public was just going to complicate everything. Cassie glanced at Whitney, who was smugly smiling at all the girls who were sitting on the edge of their seats, waiting to be named Nate's mate and actually expecting him to do so.

"Cassie passing her exam last Friday was enough for me to realize she is the one." Nate was interrupted by the blonde at the very front of the room.

"If that was all you were waiting for, I'd have taken it last week also. You should have told us. I'm sure there's more than one person here that would gladly take the exam to be considered for your mate," Jess said as she stood. Several girls nodded along with her.

"I wasn't waiting for anything and that wasn't the requirement. It was seeing how she was brave enough to do something the rest of you chose not to do made her stand out a bit," Nate continued. "In all honesty, I kind of have felt for years that I'd be paired with Cassie. I just needed to wait until she joined the coven to do so."

Cassie slid down in her seat. It was bad enough when people whispered about her when she was in earshot, but these guys were outright having a conversation.

"But it's not fair," Jess continued to complain.

Nate moved faster than a blink and was immediately in front of Jess. She jumped at his sudden appearance, and for once, instead of the smug, superior look she normally wore in class, she seemed frightened. Cassie glanced from Jess to Nate and saw his blue eyes almost glowing. Cassie didn't fear Nate, but it wasn't the same for everyone else. It was kind of strange. For all the years she had been teased by these people, she never knew how much they seemed to dislike her.

"A bit of advice for Jess and anyone else in the room that would care to tell me how to live my life. I may not be in charge yet, but I will be someday. It would be best for you if you kept your opinions to yourself if you want to stick around." Nate stared directly at Jess, and she shrank back into her seat. "No matter who your mother is."

Nate casually walked back to the aisle and began climbing the steps to leave. He stopped at Cassie's row and motioned for her to come with him. She turned to Whitney, who nodded to her.

"I'm sure you'll all welcome her into the coven and clan with open arms," Nate added before opening the door to leave.

Nate reached back and took Cassie's hand to pull her into the hallway with him. The doors clanged shut behind them with everyone still frozen in their seats. Well, everyone except for Whitney, who was grinning like a cat who just caught a mouse. She enjoyed the show, probably a bit too much.

"Sorry about all of that. I know this has all been kept from you, but it hasn't from them. A little power can make even the nicest person a bit crazy," Nate explained, not letting go of Cassie's hand.

Cassie hated herself for not pulling her hand back from him either. His hand was warm and soft. She was more than sure the anger back in the room was directed at her, but holding onto Nate made her feel safe.

"I'm really sorry about Saturday night. I could have handled it better. I never knew Jess would go that far," Nate apologized again.

That wasn't like him. Searching her mind, she couldn't remember a time Nate had apologized for anything in the past eight years. She could vividly remember the last time when she was seven and the first time she was teased about not having parents. He was sorry he was late and not there to protect her.

Cassie shrugged. Jess hadn't liked her before Nate broke up with her. He was just one more reason in a long line for that anger.

"I know you don't understand all of this, and again I feel bad for that. I never wanted to keep the night human world from you, but my father decided it was better that way. He was worried your father wasn't a skinwalker, and you were possibly sent to ruin us. John had him convinced the best thing to do was to keep it all from you. That was never my choice. Your friends had orders also to keep everything from you. They were just following them."

Nate was now defending her friends. Cassie gawked at him. Where was the jerk she was used to?

"If you'd let me make it up to you, I'd like to take you out on a date. Like a real date with just the two of us," he continued.

Cassie looked up at him. The blue glow in his eyes was now muted, but they were still just as beautiful as he stared at her. He was completely serious. He reached up and hesitantly touched her face, his thumb tracing the line from her ear to her jaw. Just that simple motion made Cassie's heartbeat pick up. He leaned forward slowly. He was going to kiss her again, and Cassie was unable to stop it.

"She'd love to," Whitney answered for Cassie as she cracked the door open farther. "But right now we need to head over to the library before they realize I'm not coming back to the room."

Cassie snapped out of the fuzzy feelings Nate was giving her. He wasn't being a jerk for the moment, but that didn't change anything. She wanted to be able to choose her own life, and a prearranged mate wasn't her idea of choosing.

Whitney looped her arm in Cassie's before pulling her the other direction.

"Wait." Nate stopped them before they could get away. He pulled a necklace out of his pocket. "If you wear this all the girly hate stuff should stop."

Cassie looked at the flat, quarter-sized pendant. There were markings on it, but nothing she recognized as meaning anything. She glanced at Whitney, who nodded to her. After undoing the clasp, Nate held it up to put on Cassie. Letting go of her friend, she took the two steps back to him. He walked behind her, and she pulled up her hair as he clasped it behind her, brushing his fingers on her neck.

"Friday night work for you?" he asked. Cassie turned and looked at him. His eyes were sparkling again, and she couldn't help but stare.

"Friday night?" Cassie wanted to know what he was asking, but his eyes were too distracting.

"That works fine," Whitney said, cutting in and pulling Cassie away from Nate.

"You got the first shift?" Nate asked Whitney.

"If you can get me out of witch classes," she replied.

Nate gave her a curt nod, and Whitney nodded back. Cassie was still reprimanding herself for getting caught up with him again. She wanted her freedom, but when she was alone with him, it was hard to keep her wits about her. He had some sort of pull on her, and she needed her aunt back … now.

Cassie stared outside the library, watching the birds as they stepped around the low branches of the tree just within feet of the window. One of the little birds found a patch of berries and chirped to get the attention of the others. Soon the branches were filled with birds all eating away. Their lives seemed much more inviting than her own at the moment. Cassie and Whitney still hadn't found a way to sneak access to the books they needed, and they had been at the library all week trying. It was already Friday, and the ceremony was a week away. Cassie needed to get her aunt home, and she needed the key to figure out how to get out of the bonding.

The worst part of everything was that Nate was being nice to her all the time. She still saw his jerk moments to others, but to her, he was being normal Nate. He was making it harder and harder to hate him.

"I think Mrs. Elms is going to be on shift tonight. If we have any chance, it's with her around. She's half blind, and I don't think they ever give her the right glasses," Whitney said as she sat back down. "I'm pretty sure I just saw her come in. If we give them a few minutes, they should be changing who sits at the reference desk."

Cassie nodded to her friend. She had to hope she was right. The ceremony was getting closer every day, and she was running out of options. Without telling Whitney, Cassie already packed a bag at her uncle's house. She didn't have anywhere she could go, but Cassie refused to just sit by and be married off.

"I'm going to go see if I can get the books. Have your bags ready, and we'll run as soon as I get them." Whitney stood up and headed to the information desk.

Cassie watched her friend turn the corner to leave. Quickly, she packed up her bag and hoped today would be the day they finally got the books. They were going to have to search for other options if they didn't.

"This seat taken?" a male voice asked from behind Cassie.

She kept packing her bag with her face down as she replied, "Nope, just leaving."

Seeing the chair next to her being pulled out, she looked up. There was a teenage boy with dark brown hair and the same honey brown eyes as her sitting down in the seat next to her. Cassie had never seen the boy before, yet he looked familiar.

"You go to Atwood High?" he asked.

"Yeah. And you?" She knew just about everyone at her school. This boy was definitely not from her high school, but she had no other reply.

"No. Homeschooled," he answered. He glanced up at the way Whitney had gone. A second guy stood there and held up two fingers. "Cassie, right?"

Cassie grabbed her bag and quickly stood. She surely didn't know the guy, yet he knew her name. And he was there with someone else—his lookout.

"Sorry." The teen held up his hands. "I didn't intend to startle you. I mean you no harm. I'm here because we're family. I know you probably think I'm crazy, but I promise you that I'm your cousin. I'm going to reach into my pocket now and take out a picture. It will prove it to you."

He slowly reached into his front pants pocket. If he was going to cast a spell on her, there wouldn't have been enough room in his pocket to hide it, nor was there room for any weapons. Cassie relaxed a little as he pulled out a folded piece of paper. The guy set it on the table and slid it in Cassie's direction.

"My name's Jack. I'm the son of your Uncle Michael," Jack explained.

"I don't have an Uncle Michael." She didn't take her eyes off the guy named Jack as she took the paper from the table.

"I don't have time to debate that with you," Jack replied,

glancing at his friend who was waving him to leave. "That picture proves to you I'm telling the truth. My father is the one next to John. Next time I see you here, you'll know the truth, hopefully. And if the skinwalkers won't tell you about the wendigo, I will. Be safe around them. They can't be trusted, and neither can the coven. All they want is your power. Our family line is one of the first, and they know that."

Jack didn't even say good-bye when he left, following his friend in the opposite direction as Whitney was now coming from. Cassie didn't know why, but she quickly put the picture in her pocket. It wasn't that she didn't trust Whitney—she did, completely—it was just that it seemed like there was maybe more Cassie wanted to know that Whitney wouldn't be allowed to tell her. She had already gotten her friend in enough trouble, and if the alpha really could read her mind, Cassie needed to be careful.

Whitney walked carefully toward Cassie, concealing the bulge of books in her shirt. She mouthed the words *got it* before she made it to the table. Cassie quickly grabbed her bag and Whitney's before following her friend to one of the far corners of the library. Whitney paused to listen around them before she plopped down on the floor. Cassie sat beside her.

"This would be much easier in a week. Then they couldn't restrict your access to those books. Once you're part of the coven, you can learn anything you want to," Whitney commented.

"If I become part of it," Cassie corrected.

Whitney rolled her eyes. "If Maria could figure out how to get out of the bond, then you can, too. Besides, you can't leave me. Do you know how much it would suck to be the only one people avoid around here?"

Cassie couldn't help but smile. Learning about the skinwalkers had taught her why even though her friend was more beautiful than most of the girls in the school, and had just as great a personality to go with her looks, no one would be friends with her. It wasn't just unusual for a skinwalker to be born female; it was close to rare, with less than ten ever recorded being born. It also meant that unless a male witch was born that they didn't know about, Whitney wouldn't even have a mate to be bonded to. A female skinwalker wasn't someone anyone wanted to get close with. Some even started the rumor at her old school that she was cursed, and that was why she was born the way she was. Whitney never looked at it as a curse, but she hated it anyway.

"It should be in one of these books," Whitney said as she split the stack she pilfered in half. "We have to be quick; I promised Than you'd be home and ready by four."

"Four?" Cassie asked. It was Friday night, and Nate wanted to pick her up at four. Cassie hadn't been on any dates before, but she did know that most didn't start that early.

"He wanted to pick you up right from school, but then I told him we'd be here again," Whitney explained, taking the book onto her lap.

"Or you could just lose me on the way home, and I could hide in my room all night," Cassie suggested. "Better yet, take me home with you and I can hide in your room all night. That sounds like even more fun. Sam won't tell on me, and your parents aren't home." Sam idolized his big sister and would probably jump at the chance to help them.

Whitney laughed. "Not a chance. I'd have to deal with Than in my head all the time. It's been bad enough already with him constantly bugging me about you; I don't think I could stand hours of him sifting through my memories night after night."

"He wouldn't."

"Already has," Whitney replied, cracking open the top book on her stack. "The night you went missing. He was bound and determined to find you. He sifted through all my memories to find the cabin you were in."

"But I never took you there," Cassie commented. "And you said they can't see me in your memories."

"But you did tell me about it. I went looking for the cabin once during a night run to see it for myself. Once he found that memory, he was able to focus on finding you." Whitney paged through her book, and Cassie opened hers to do the same.

"Besides, that mark doesn't just mark you as his own; it gives him a way to find you, or you him."

"What?" Cassie asked a little too loudly, glancing up from her book.

Whitney quickly looked around again.

"Shh. Do you want to be discovered before we can get the spell to find your aunt?" Whitney scolded.

"What did you mean he can find me?" Cassie asked, quieter this time.

"That mark shows you are connected. He can use it to find you, or you him. Don't ask me how. I don't have one," Whitney explained, shutting her first book and opening the second.

Cassie opened her book but didn't look too hard at it. She paged through the spells, but thought about how Nate could find her. Did that mean if she had to leave he would find her? Was Cassie really trapped unless they could find Aunt Maria? It wasn't looking good the more she learned. Cassie paged through the whole book without finding anything that would help.

"Cool," Whitney said. Cassie shut her book and crawled over next to her friend.

"Did you find it?" she asked, looking down at the spell. How to locate a lost pet. Not something that would help.

"Oh, sorry. I had this cat as a child that we never found after she got out. If I had this spell, we would have been able to find her. I'll have to keep this in mind. We've lost more than one pet over the years."

"And you do know my aunt isn't a pet," Cassie added

with a little more attitude than she meant to. Whitney looked up, startled by her best friend's tone.

"Sorry. I know I'm supposed to be looking for her. I haven't found a thing yet," Whitney added as she began to page through the book more. Cassie crawled back over to her side of the hiding spot.

"Sorry," Cassie immediately apologized.

"Not a problem. I'd be stressed out, too, if I were in your shoes. Well, maybe not. Than is kind of nice to look at. I bet he's even better to kiss."

Whitney stared dreamily into space. Cassie shook her head. It did seem like she should just take the chance that fate knew what it was doing, but that wasn't Cassie. She didn't like being told what to do.

"It's just that I don't want to have to leave," Cassie complained. There was nothing in any of the books Cassie had. Dread was beginning to settle in. She might not be finding Aunt Maria after all.

"I don't want you to leave, either. I swear we'll keep at this until we find an answer," Whitney added. "Maybe your uncle can help."

Cassie wondered about that also. He seemed to still be in a better mood now that Cassie knew everything, but she wasn't sure if he would be willing to help her, or if he even could. Then there was the picture in her pocket. Cassie needed to look at that better and see who this Jack person was.

Whitney glanced at her phone and nodded to herself. "We need to get you back home. An hour should be enough time to get ready."

"Or I could just show up like this. We still have time," Cassie added. She didn't want to give up.

"What is it about being bonded to him that you don't like?" Whitney asked, standing up and picking up the books, signaling she was finished.

"In reality," Cassie began, then paused, "it isn't just him.

I don't want to be bonded to anyone right now. I'm only sixteen. I shouldn't have to make a life decision like that. How crazy is this night human world? I'm still a child. I mean, I've had my driver's license for less than a year, so why not go get married?"

Whitney laughed. "I can only imagine how odd that seems to you. For me, it's always been like that. We are raised knowing that we're supposed to find our partner in our teen years. It may seem weird, but I can't knock it. It also seems to work."

"You mean besides my aunt, there isn't anyone else bonded to someone they don't want to be with?"

Whitney took Cassie's books before heading back to the main section of the library.

"Actually, no. No one I know is unhappy with the bond. From what I hear, the bond won't even work unless you both want it," Whitney added. "Since you don't want it, it is possible that you could do the ceremony and join the coven without being bonded. Maybe that's how Maria got around it."

Cassie followed her friend. She doubted it was that easy. She had already told Nate she didn't want to be with him, and yet, everyone claimed his mark was on her neck. No matter how many times she told him to go away or that she wasn't going to be his mate, the mark didn't disappear. It didn't seem to be as easy as just refusing.

CHAPTER 8

The miniskirt Whitney had picked out was way too short. Cassie wasn't a skirt girl to begin with, but an itty-bitty jean skirt was a bit much. Whitney insisted it made Cassie seem more innocent, but she wasn't sure that was the vibe she wanted to give off.

Cassie's mind was elsewhere when Nate pulled up to the house. John paced around the room, more anxious than she was.

The photo Jack had given her sure did look like her mother, Uncle John, Aunt Maria, and someone else, but it wasn't hard to use Photoshop. Cassie needed time to search the house for the original. She was sure she had seen the picture without the mysterious possible-uncle before; she just didn't know where. She did think to ask her Uncle John, but after asking him about Maria and getting him upset once already, Cassie didn't want to take her chances.

Nate arrived right at four. He knocked on the door, but before he could take a step back, John was there. Nate walked in, and John stood toe-to-toe with him, each staring down the other. Nate didn't blink, looking at her massive uncle. It wasn't like Nate was small himself, but Uncle John was simply intimidating. Her aunt used to tease that he had been born intimidating.

Cassie stepped between the guys, forcing their staring contest to end. She wanted to get the date over with and get back home to search the house for the photo. John was in complete fall mode and would be asleep by seven and unwakeable for hours.

"Her curfew is eleven," John said as Nate held out his hand for Cassie.

It sucked that the mating bond made her hand move toward his and take it into her own.

"Of course, Mr. Booth. I will have her back by 10:55."

John nodded to Nate as he led Cassie away. She wished he had been nicer and more helpful when she questioned him earlier about breaking the temporary mating bond to get out of the permanent one, but he was just as stressed about all of it as she was. She had put him in that disposition.

"Why's he moody today?" Nate opened Cassie's door for her.

"I asked him how my aunt got out of the bond," Cassie answered. She said she would go on a date with Nate. She never said she would play nice.

After closing her door, he went around to the driver's side.

"Well, that would do it," Nate replied, not even deterred by what Cassie was trying to do.

Nate started up his car. It was a fancy black sports car. Cassie had heard his parents got it for him for his sixteenth birthday last year, which didn't surprise her much. They had the money, and indulging their one and only son was one of their favorite ways to spend it.

"It's kind of a touchy subject with him," Nate replied.

"I'd say," Cassie replied. She already figured that one out the hard way.

"When your aunt chose not to bond, it upset the balance of the group. For each skinwalker, there's a witch, and for each witch a skinwalker. If we get one more on either side, then there isn't a partner for someone. When Maria backed out, that meant we had too many skinwalkers. John gave up his chance for a mate for her to go without one. He will never have a witch counterpart and the only reason he can still be here is because he was next in line to be alpha. His power keeps him stable."

"Stable?" Cassie asked. No one had explained this part of it to her yet.

"Whitney said she was teaching you all this stuff when you guys left school," Nate replied.

Did she? Cassie wasn't sure what she was supposed to be faking now.

"I figured it was just an excuse to hang out with you," Nate chuckled, catching Cassie without a response.

"So the witch for a skinwalker, skinwalker for a witch thing," Cassie said, getting Nate away from the topic of Whitney and what they'd been doing every afternoon for the past week.

"We're all born in pairs." Nate drove to the park not far from her house and parked the car while they talked.

"As in, soulmates?" Cassie asked. That would have sounded romantic before she found herself mated to Nate.

"No, more like keys and locks. You can key a house to have all the same locks and all the same keys. So one house could have five locks and five keys. They all fit together, but they don't work for another house."

Cassie nodded. It made sense, but Cassie still didn't like the idea of having absolutely no choice.

"Why do the skinwalkers pair up with the witches?" Cassie asked. Whitney had told her the general ideas. Skinwalkers couldn't stand direct sunlight for long, needed blood to survive, and turned into monsters at night. Whitney also explained that skinwalkers were only one type of night human, and there were others—lots of others.

"A long time ago the skinwalkers found that their night human power was too much for the body to handle. They would change with the moons, but eventually they would change permanently into their family totem." Nate parked his car. "The first ones had families and didn't want to leave them alone, so they chose to fight the change. But the change didn't come easy. It's a very painful process, and to go through it forcibly once a month took its toll. Many of the first skinwalkers went crazy. That's when the women of the skinwalkers looked for a way to help. They found it in the form of witch magic. By combining day human witch magic with night human skinwalkers, it made the process painless."

"So basically, you want to bind to me to take away your pain from changing into a night human?"

"No ... yes ... No ... I don't know." Nate ran his hands through his almost black hair, his favorite nervous move. "No. That isn't the reason I want to bind to you. Yes, it would help with the change and the pain of changing among other things. But no, I didn't even consider that when I kissed you at the dance. I wasn't trying to bind you to me or make you choose me. I just felt like I had to kiss you."

Cassie had to hold her giggle in. She had never seen him flustered before. It just made him cuter than he already was.

"What did the witches get out of the binding?" Cassie asked. "I understand that the first ones got to keep their husbands and whatnot. But what about everyone one beyond that? I mean, here everyone expects us to bind our lives together, and we don't even really know each other. What does a witch get out of binding someone they don't even know?"

Nate seemed taken back by the question.

"You know me, Cassie. We've been friends for close to forever."

"I knew you, Nate. Knew. I don't know you now. Remember when you decided you were too good to hang out with Owen and me? That was almost eight years ago. We aren't the same kids now."

"I never said that. I had to join them. That was when your uncle gave up being next in line to my father. That's when I was chosen to be the next alpha. I didn't ask to be popular. I didn't want to get a whole new group of friends. I wanted to stay with you and Owen, but my father forbade it. He was too worried that you weren't of skinwalker blood," Nate explained.

He was begging Cassie to forgive him with his eyes as he talked.

"You can't bind to someone you don't know," he continued, giving her puppy dog eyes. "It doesn't work that way. For the magic to choose for us to be together lots of things had to be in line. We had to be compatible, power-wise. I was never going to be able to bind anyone I chose. They had to be able to handle the power of my totem. Second, you have to know each other and want to be bonded. My mark would have never shown up on you if you didn't want me as much as I wanted you. You can tell everyone else that you don't want to be with me, but I know better," Nate replied. "That's how the bond works."

Cassie crossed her arms and stared out the window.

"You still haven't explained what I get out of it," she answered. She couldn't deny what he had said. He was the only one that knew she had kissed him back.

"When we bind, you gain access to my totem also. You can make me transform on command, and you can use any of the power behind it. You won't ever get sick again. You will heal just as quickly as a skinwalker. You can temporarily be faster and stronger. You can use my power to do all sorts of stuff. And you will be part of the coven. Isn't that what you always wanted? Do you not want that now?"

Cassie didn't look at him. He had a point, and she didn't want him to know he was right.

Nate started the car back up. He didn't need to say anything. He had won the argument, but that didn't change anything. Cassie still wanted to be the one making her choices, not fate.

Driving in silence, Nate made his way back through town. Cassie could already tell where he was going. As kids, she had spent many hours with him and Owen at his family's estate in the country. Nate didn't stop at the house, but continued to drive farther to the back. He parked next to the immaculately kept barn.

"You always loved the horses." Nate turned off the car, and before Cassie had a chance to open her door, he was already around to her side.

Cassie stepped out even though she was still mad about losing the argument. It had been years since she had been to the stables.

"Sadie Mare is still here," Nate said as he opened the side door into the barn.

Cassie smiled, remembering the old chestnut mare that was always her favorite.

"We don't ride her anymore, but she keeps the younger ones in line," he told Cassie, reaching for her hand. Every cell in her body ached to hold his hand, just to touch him.

Cassie took his hand easily and let him lead the way, even though she remembered quite well where the old horse would be. Nate stopped at the half wall and peered into the stall. There was the old girl Cassie had grown to love as her favorite. Sadie came right over to Cassie and whinnied. Reaching up with her free hand, Cassie touched the horse's nose. She was still soft.

"Hi, girl," Cassie murmured. Sadie nudged Cassie's hand to be stroked more. "It's been a while."

"I knew she would remember you," Nate commented, reaching up and petting her with his free hand also.

Cassie couldn't help but smile. They had spent so much of their free time in the barn running around. The boys loved to play hide and seek, but Cassie preferred to just sit and watch the horses. There was something calming about them.

"I'll bring her back to you later," Nate told the old horse. She neighed at him, like she understood.

"She's not afraid of you, even though you turn into a ..." Cassie was unsure what to call him. Whitney turned into a cat at night. She didn't know what Nate was.

"No. She knows the difference between good and bad night humans. Most animals do," Nate explained.

"And you're the good kind?"

"Of course." Nate led the way to the stairs and the loft.

"So what kind are you?" Cassie asked, her interest piqued.

"That you have to guess," Nate replied as they made their way to the top of the stairs.

The extra hay bales were artfully arranged and blankets spread on them to make a table and chairs. The red checkered table had a large basket on it.

"I figured I could take you out to Almira's, and we would be stared at as we go on our first date, or we could just have a picnic here. You've been stared at enough for several lifetimes. This was the quieter option and most like you." Nate seemed as if he was waiting for her approval.

He was right, she didn't need to be taken to the most expensive restaurant in town. In fact, she pretty much was sure to not enjoy that. Maybe she hadn't changed much, but he had. And Cassie needed to remember that.

Nate motioned for her to sit down. After doing so, Cassie waited as Nate began to unload the basket.

"So, what animal are you?" she asked again as she watched.

"Technically, since you aren't part of the coven, I can't tell you," Nate replied, opening the containers he took out. "Just like we didn't technically tell you what your uncle was. You guessed that."

"So they want me to bond to you and share power with you, but not know what you are?"

Nate nodded as Cassie gawked at all the food he had pulled out. She was glad for once that her stomach didn't choose that moment to growl at all the delicious-looking food.

"But that's not fair." Her mouth watered when he opened the next container. "I mean, what if you were like a salamander? How much power could a little two-inch salamander share with a person?"

Nate laughed, and Cassie smiled. It was nice to hear his

laugh again. It had been a long time since she saw him smile as much as he had already since he picked her up, but laughing was completely unheard of with the great Than Bay. He was stoic and serious. He wasn't the smiling or laughing kind of person now.

"Well, rest assured I'm not a salamander," Nate replied. "In fact, I'm pretty sure no one is a salamander. We tend to be larger and a bit more ferocious."

"So you are all carnivores?" Cassie inquired as he handed her a bowl of food. She took it without asking what kind of pasta it was. Even as kids he could cook. She was sure it must be a night human thing now that she knew her uncle was one also.

"Mmm." Nate thought as he chewed. "Yeah, I think we all are. We don't have to be, but right now I think all the ones in our coven are."

"So there are other covens and skinwalkers?" Cassie asked. She was way too new to it all.

"Yes, we currently have six covens with skinwalkers," Nate explained, taking another bite.

Again, this was news to Cassie. She had only learned the basics about their coven, but she understood now. They all assumed, according to her uncle, that she wasn't one of them. She'd need her father to prove that, but since she took the exam, that seemed to be proof enough.

"So Whitney came from another one?" Cassie asked. Her friend had moved to town in middle school. Everyone else Cassie knew was born and raised in town.

"Yeah. Her coven should have had a male born with powers, but since they didn't, she came here to wait until one of the covens has a male witch."

"So Whitney has no counterpart?" Cassie both felt sad for her friend and hopeful that it meant something.

"The coven always has balance. I'm sure there must be a male witch around for her; he just hasn't come into his powers yet," Nate explained.

"Then why'd she come here?"

"Because we're in charge of all the covens. I'm not just next in line to be alpha for this coven, but for all of them," Nate explained.

Cassie tried not to show her shock by reaching for the dessert. Averting her eyes, she avoided his gaze. It was chocolate pie; her favorite.

"So you must be a very strong animal," Cassie continued her guessing game.

"I suppose," Nate replied with a shrug.

"Come on. Can't you just tell me?"

"Nope." Nate reached forward and took a swipe of the whipped cream on her pie.

"Hey, get your own, buddy," Cassie teased, pulling it away from him and eating the whipped cream all in one mouthful. "Come on. Can't you give me a hint? I mean ... sure you can't tell me, but can't you like act it out or something?"

"Act it out?"

Nate laughed again. It was a good sound, and had been so long missing. He had been one of her best friends once, and somewhere inside of him that guy was still trapped, it seemed. Cassie hated that he was still there. It was much easier to hate the jerk he had become.

"Fine."

Nate stood up. He moved silently across the barn and back again. Slowly he turned, and his blue eyes glowed in the slightly dark corner he was standing in.

"When I hunt, I like to stalk my prey like this. Close your eyes."

Cassie looked skeptically at him.

"Please," he added.

Cassie couldn't refuse him being nice.

"Fine," she fake protested as she closed her eyes.

"I'm an animal that can walk silently," Nate said from farther away on her left side. "And get close without anyone knowing." His voice was right outside her right side. She lifted her arms to touch him and felt the whoosh of air where he moved away.

She could hear the horses below as they moved and neighed, but not Nate. He was more than silent. He was a ghost. Cassie felt a warm hand caress the side of her face. She turned to open her eyes to him, but there was no one there. Now, with her eyes open, she looked around. He shouldn't be able to hide in his dark jeans and red top amongst the tan hay bales, but she had no clue where he was. Cassie had scanned around her before she felt the whoosh of another touch to her cheek, this time the opposite side. She turned in the other direction, now circling around counterclockwise. Nate had vanished.

Cassie stood and walked over to the loose hay. Maybe he was hiding. She leaned on a bale of hay and looked around for the third time. He had just vanished.

"You've proven your point," she said to the empty loft.

Cassie felt the hit to her middle before she saw him. Nate grinned as they fell into the soft yet crunchy hay. He tilted their bodies so that he took the brunt of the fall, and Cassie landed on him, giggling.

"So your totem is a ninja gecko?" Cassie teased.

"Sure. We're all a bunch of ninja lizards in our clan." Nate laughed, pulling straw from Cassie's hair.

She gazed up into his eyes as they peered back at her. They were questioning her. It had been such a long time since she'd had that much fun with Nate. Years, to be exact.

"I've missed you greatly," Nate said quietly as he leaned closer. He paused only centimeters from her face.

Cassie didn't think before meeting him in the middle of the space between them. It was like her body had a mind of its own, or maybe it was her heart. His lip met hers, and the feeling was as wonderful as the other night at the dance. Something about kissing Nate felt just right, or more to be exact, it felt perfect. Cassie pulled back to catch her breath.

Nate grinned at her. "Now do you see how perfect we are together? Fate wouldn't let a kiss be that great for no reason."

Nate's words brought Cassie back to reality. Quickly, she pushed herself up and got some distance from the supernatural pull that made her want to jump back into his arms. Cassie hugged herself as she suddenly felt cold. Concern lacing his face, Nate gracefully stood and reached to pull her back to himself. Cassie took a step away to keep her head clear. It was like as soon as he touched her; she wanted nothing but him. It was magic interfering with her life. She didn't want that.

"Cas, I didn't mean to upset you." Nate held his hands up in surrender.

"It's not you. I just don't like all this fate stuff. I want to be in control of my life. I didn't even get a say in whether that mark appeared on me. I want a choice in all of this."

"You get a say," Nate tried to reassure her.

"When? From what I've been told, either I join the coven as your mate, or I leave," Cassie replied. Nate looked taken aback by her options.

"You're going to leave?" he asked; surprise still showed on his face.

"I don't know what I'm going to do, but two weeks sure isn't a long enough time to agree to be someone's mate. From what I've been told, night humans mate for *life*." Cassie emphasized the word life. She needed Nate to see that everything had gotten way too serious too quickly.

"Cas," Nate walked forward slowly, "I know this is all new to you, but I promise you, this was never just a quick decision. I've been hoping since we were kids that you'd end up being part-skinwalker. I've had a crush on you for practically forever. Then my father made me stop hanging out with you guys. I always thought I'd have to beat Owen to be with you. I never once thought you'd choose me."

"But that's just it. I didn't choose anyone," Cassie

replied, exasperated that no one, especially Nate, had faith in her.

"I know you don't believe it, but you did choose me. How many guys have you kissed before?" Nate asked, only a little jealously tingeing his question. Part of Cassie wanted to lie and see how mad that might make him.

Cassie turned away. Her real answer was beyond embarrassing. How could she be out kissing guys when, in the first place, she was considered a social outcast? It wasn't like the guys were all trying to go out with her, except for the dance. And second, her uncle would never let her date. This was the first official date she was ever let on, and that was only because Uncle John couldn't say no to Nate. Nate had to know her answer.

Cassie walked back to the dinner that was now over. It had been perfect for a moment.

"Can you just take me home?" she asked.

Nate walked up beside her, his hands raised to touch her, but he pulled them back to his side.

"Yes, but I'm not finished showing you that I'm the right night human for you. The ceremony isn't for one week. That's enough time to convince you to choose me," Nate told her, his cocky self back in place.

Cassie sat up at the slight tap on her door. She had been home frantically trying to get ahold of Whitney for two hours. When her best friend didn't call back, Cassie thought a nap would help her. It was easy to fall asleep since she hadn't been sleeping well for the past week.

"Come in," Cassie said, expecting her friend to finally be there.

Uncle John walked into the room cautiously.

"Oh." Cassie attempted to hide her disappointment as much as she could. "Hi, John."

"Hey, Cassie. I wanted to let you know I'm leaving for

my Friday meeting with the clan," John said.

"That's where you go every Friday?" Cassie replied. "I always thought it was strange when you told me you were in a bowling league. I couldn't picture you bowling."

Cassie laughed. She could remember the exact moment when she asked her uncle where he was going one time as a kid. Aunt Maria had just showed up to babysit, and Cassie wanted to go with Uncle John.

John laughed, too. "Hey, it was the best excuse I could give you. And after that one time we took you bowling and you hated it, I figured it was the only way to keep you from asking to go with us again."

"Well, it worked. I thought you going bowling was strange, but I sure didn't want to go with you. No Aunt Maria to babysit this time?" Cassie asked, hopefully. It had been years since Maria had been needed to babysit, but Cassie could be hopeful.

"No, sorry. I still can't get ahold of her. I'm trying, but I have the feeling that some people are keeping her from us," John replied without any real clues, but Cassie could read between the lines.

"I've heard," Cassie muttered bitterly.

"But you do have a few babysitters of sorts downstairs now," John added, running his hands through his dark longer hair that was curling at the edges. He needed Maria back for a haircut if nothing else.

"Babysitters?" Cassie asked suspiciously.

"Five of your classmates from school are sticking around to keep things safe while I'm gone," John explained.

"Safe? Or is that a secret I'm not allowed to know either?"

"They're worried that since you were found to be a match for Nate that other night humans will want to steal you to be theirs. He's a powerful kid, and to be his mate makes you his equal. It's not often you find that in someone so young. It's why I kept you from them. I knew it all along." John shrugged. "Anyway. Keep your door shut and it's probably best to set a few spells around the room also. I don't doubt Nate can keep them in line, but better be safe than sorry."

"In line?" Cassie asked. She had already seen tons of them the night they surrounded the cabin.

"Younger they are, the harder it is to control the urge to feed off humans when in the between form. It's almost gone when you're a full animal, but hard in the part animal phase," Uncle John explained. "Please stay safe and in your room all night. If you need anything, go get it now. You have a few minutes before I leave."

Cassie nodded and walked over to her uncle. He looked so defeated. Cassie might have not understood all the years that she felt rejected, but she knew now. He was just trying to keep her from everything. She wished she had known. She reached out and hugged him before he could leave.

"Everything will work out, kiddo. I swear. You won't have to do anything you don't want to do. I'll make sure of it," he promised, whispering the words against her head.

"Don't worry about it. We'll find a way to get Maria home. Whit's helping me."

"There's more than just me that doesn't like the system," John added. "Now get your treats and get those spells set. I don't want our problem solved by something happening to you."

"I love you, Uncle John." Cassie gave him one last squeeze.

"Yeah, yeah, kiddo." John patted her head as she let go.

Cassie smiled up at him as he led the way back down the stairs. He tried not to show that he needed the hug, but Cassie knew. This was almost as hard for him as it was for her.

Passing the living room, she didn't even look inside it. Cassie didn't care who was there. She already knew Nate was; she had felt it when he arrived a moment before. After her hands were filled with snacks, she went back upstairs for the night. She had a bathroom, treats, and a TV. She would be set. Before she closed the door, she set spells around the room. She hoped her uncle was right about Nate keeping the monsters away.

"Cassie," someone said from outside the door.

Cassie hurried over and opened the door. Just outside of her spell stood Whitney. Cassie had thought the voice didn't sound like a guy.

"Sorry I didn't call you back. We've been a bit busy. I had to sit through a full clan meeting about next week, and then an additional meeting about tonight. So how'd it go?" she asked, sitting down outside the spell to keep night humans out of her room.

Cassie sat on her side of the barrier.

"How'd it go?" Whitney asked a second time, trying to curb her eagerness, but not doing a good job.

Cassie didn't know how to reply.

"That bad?" Whitney prodded.

"It was good up to a point. I think I just don't fit in here," Cassie replied. "I mean. I know this is my family, and I want to be part of the coven, but I dunno. I don't fit. How come I can't just accept this like everyone tells me I should?"

"Hey, this isn't your fault. Nate never should have kissed you. We should have had time to explain all of this. I get the whole two weeks thing, but they should have given you more options. You just learned about all of this. This is all the fault of the clan. This isn't your fault." Whitney pushed against the barrier as she reached to hug Cassie, and then laughed as she pulled back.

"Do you know how much it sucks to be on this side of the barrier?" Whitney asked. "I've spent my whole life wishing to be in your shoes, but right now I'm pretty sure I wouldn't want to be. I don't want you to leave me. You're the only normal person I know. I'm sorry we haven't been able to get Maria yet. I promise we'll find her."

"I hope so," Cassie replied.

Whitney stood. "Time for me to join the freaks downstairs."

"I wish you didn't have to go," Cassie complained. She really needed her best friend.

"I wish I didn't either," Whitney replied. "Maybe you could do that wish spell and wish me to change into my full animal. Then I could join you."

"Sure. We can give that a try," Cassie replied.

Shutting her door, Cassie went back into her bag of potions. Quickly, she found the two spells she needed and added them together. She wished to see her friend as a fuzzy tiger. She didn't want to be alone. Cassie doubted it would work. Their breed of magic was way stronger than a simple wish spell, but it didn't hurt to try.

Soon enough there was scratching at the door. Cassie would have worried about opening it, but she already knew her protection spell would keep the monsters downstairs out as Whitney demonstrated. All she could hope was that her spell would let the furry version of her friend in.

Cassie opened the door, and the large striped tiger pushed the door open farther with her nose. Cassie ran her hand down the tiger's back as she walked by. Tiger Whitney paused while Cassie shut the door. Once she had, the tiger sat down at the bed and waited with a thumping tail for Cassie to join her.

"Impatient?" she asked, smiling.

The tiger huffed and nodded to the door.

"The wards are all set," she told her friend who was staring at the door still. "Promise. No one else is getting in. You could only get through in your furry state."

Cassie walked over to her dresser. "I'm gonna change before opening the snacks." Cassie grabbed her pajamas then headed to the bathroom. When she came back out, the tiger was already ripping apart one bag of chips.

"Gosh, hungry much?"

Her tiger friend looked up at her with blue eyes and gave

her a toothy grin.

"Fine. Let me get those."

Cassie reached down and grabbed the bag to open.

"Do your tastes change also when you grow fur?"

Tiger Whitney was grabbing the sour cream and onion chips. Person Whitney would never be caught eating something that could make your breath stink like that.

"This is going to be a long night without you talking back. How am I supposed to get advice from you about everything?"

Pausing in her munching of the chips, Tiger Whitney looked up at Cassie and nodded.

"I suppose that's the best I'll get from you. You know, why couldn't you turn into a talking tiger? I mean, come on, you turn into a gigantic animal at night. Why not a gigantic talking animal? It would make my life easier ... but I guess there isn't anything easy in my fate cards these days."

Cassie sat down on her bed. Soon enough the tiger was done eating and jumped up next to her. She stretched beside Cassie, taking up more than most of the bed. The tiger yawned before nudging the pillow next to her. Lying down, Cassie put her head on her pillow.

"You know the worst part of the date?" Cassie asked; the tiger lifted her head to look at Cassie. "It was actually fun. For the first and only date I've ever been on, it was the best I've had. I mean, the only comparison I have is your date, but I promise you it was much better."

The tiger nudged Cassie with her forehead.

"No way are you getting details out of me," Cassie added, pushing her friend's head off her pillow.

"Come on, you big lug. This bed can barely fit us both when you aren't a big furry animal." Cassie pushed her furry friend back on the bed to claim more space.

That made Tiger Whitney spread out even more. Cassie sighed. The tiger rotated to give Cassie a furry pillow to sleep on.

"Does this ever get any less weird?" she asked.

The tiger grumbled a chuckle that made Cassie's head bounce.

"Fine. I'll have to get used to it I guess."

Cassie rolled over and used the tiger to keep warm. It wouldn't be a long night now that her friend was there. How could she be worried about the half-monsters from before when she had a giant tiger with her? It was the most ferocious-looking thing she had ever met, but knowing it was her friend made her see she wasn't scary. Even if she couldn't talk, she was still Whitney.

It was hours later when Cassie awoke to a noise outside her window. She lifted her head off her pillow to see that tiger Whitney was gone, and her room door was open. Not that it mattered much. Her spell was still intact, and no one was upstairs.

Her room was warm, and Cassie went to the window to open it. She cracked it a little to let in a breeze before heading back to bed. It had been a strange night, and she was ready for her weekend to start. Whitney had promised they could go to the library first thing in the morning, but Cassie knew she didn't mean four a.m. Stumbling to her bed, she lay back down. It was too early, and more sleep was needed. Cassie rolled over and felt the warm spot where her tiger friend had been not too long ago.

"Night, night, Whitney," Cassie said even though her friend probably couldn't hear her.

CHAPTER 9

Cassie felt the wind in her hair as she floated in her dream. It felt nice after her room grew too warm. She could remember that she opened a window, and was thankful she had. She was in a fuzzy sleep state, but not willing to leave her bed. Reaching down to grab her covers, Cassie wished her tiger friend would be back, but she didn't know how long they stayed in their animal form at nighttime. The instant warmth would have been good with the breeze running over her.

Cassie's eyes tried to shoot open as she realized that there were no covers, and she couldn't move to reach anything. Her eyes were heavy with the feeling of magic. Someone had put a spell on her, and she felt the familiar pull of her muscles rejecting her own thoughts.

With silently chant a counter spell, she tried to undo the magic even though she had no clue what was going on, but was pretty sure she didn't want to find out by ending up on an altar somewhere. Aunt Maria used to scare Cassie with tales of witches going against each other and sacrificing each other to gain power. She hoped those were all tales.

The wind blew harder as Cassie was carried by someone, a very large someone. Her sense of smell told her it was an unclean someone, but not the person who had cast the spell.

Her eyes regained function, but she kept them closed as she chanted more in her mind. Slowly, she could feel her fingertips and then her whole fingers. Projecting her spells silently had come in handy twice in a week now. Cassie would have to thank her aunt when she finally came home.

Leaves crackled as her abductor continued to move. Beneath her hands was a blanket that she was being held in. It was the only thing keeping her warm. Hopefully, it meant they didn't want to hurt her since they had done that. Her head was being held tight against the body of the person carrying her. Soon enough, their movement stopped. Cassie felt the ground beneath her when she was set down.

She cracked her eyes open. Standing only feet away was one of the monsters she had seen before, a half-transformed skinwalker. Cassie wanted to sit up and ask them who they were and why they took her away from everyone, but something told her to keep silent. Cassie trusted her gut. It had gotten her out of more than one bad occasion.

The creature screeched, and she shivered. It was calling to others. Cassie peeked again and discovered the creature had moved farther away. She expected to be in the woods, but instead knew exactly where they were—they were just outside Miller Diner on the edge of town. The creature stalked away toward the woods behind the diner. Cassie wiggled her toes. She had feeling back in all of her body. This was her only chance since the monster walked away. She had to make it around the building and inside. There she could call for help.

She waited until the creature was farther away and had its back to her, then slowly brought her feet up to stand. Crouching on the ground, she was ready. She took a deep breath and didn't look back as she sprinted around the building. She didn't pause to listen to see if it followed her. She had a feeling it would, no matter what she tried, and she could never outrun it home. The diner was her chance.

Cassie rounded the building and slipped inside. The main door was open, but after she was inside it was too late to realize that it was still early morning. No one was in the diner, and it was closed. Cassie looked outside the half-moon window in the front door and saw the creature stalking in her direction. She took note of the empty walkway to the front door she was now trapped in. A bench was sitting there for people who would wait to be seated. It was the best she could do as she turned and pushed it against the front door. The creature noticed she was blockading herself in the diner and sprinted faster than humanly possible. Its long, clawed hands snaked inside the door and grabbed her leg. Cassie didn't pause for the pain as it broke through her skin, ripping a gash in her thigh. It was bad enough to be taken, but how Uncle John and Whitney talked about the thirst of night humans, she wouldn't live now with her blood dripping down her leg if the monster got to her. She would be too tempting not to eat. Cassie gave one last push and got the bench to stop the door from being opened.

Cassie hurried back to the other door and pounded on it. There had to be someone that came in early.

"Help," Cassie called, but there was no answer.

The creature pounded equally as hard on the front door, now unable to get inside as the bench barricaded Cassie in. It pressed its face against the window and looked at her with its red, beady eyes. Noticing the blood, the night human licked its lips.

"If we're really connected, now would be a good time to get here," Cassie muttered, rubbing the pendant she still wore from Nate.

The creature stepped back from the door and screeched again. Cassie heard the grumbling as more steps crunched across the stone parking lot. She didn't have the time or energy to peek out the window. They were slow and taking their time because she was trapped. Cassie gasped as the bench shook from the one night monster ramming the door. There was no way it was going to hold up to multiple creatures at once.

Cassie pushed against the door to the diner. She needed to get out, but her strength was slowly leaving. Blood dripped down her leg. The cut was deeper than she thought, and she was losing too much blood.

She dipped her finger in the blood. It was the last bit of power she could use, and she refused to be eaten alive by red-eyed monsters. Quickly, she drew a circle around her and anointed each compass point. She didn't have the slightest clue what would stop the creature without her potions, but it was time to improvise. The familiar hum of magic bubbled around her. At least she didn't have to die being monster food. The protection would last as long as she lasted, at least in theory.

Cassie heard a roar as more creatures arrived outside the diner. She didn't have the energy left to see what was happening, but it didn't matter. She had only minutes left before she would bleed out. The sun began to rise outside and Cassie smiled. She could see pretty red streaks lining the sky from her spot on the floor. One last sunrise.

The doors smashed open as her bench gave way. Splinters bounced off her bubble where she was lying, but she didn't have the energy to open her eyes and see her attacker.

"Cas, just stay with me," someone told her as they reached down through her magic. Even that was failing alongside her.

She felt pressure on her wound and a burning tightness. Magic she had never felt before was knitting her wound back together. Cassie wanted to see who her savior was. She was sure the voice was male. There were no male witches in the coven but magically she was being healed.

Her rescuer tipped her head back and her mouth open before she could protest. Even with a healing spell, she had still lost too much blood. They didn't have to waste their energy. She needed to know that she was fine dying. Her parents would be waiting for her on the other side.

Burning raced down her throat. The magic she felt on her wound was now inside of her, making every last part of her reenergized. Cassie felt weak, but she also felt better. She cracked open her eyes to look up at her savior. His beautiful blue eyes stared back at her. Nate held her in his arms like a baby, relief written all over his face.

"I thought I was too late." He touched his forehead to hers.

"Too late?" Cassie rasped. She was still unsure what had happened.

"I thought when I smelled all your blood that I couldn't save you," Nate replied.

"You did that magic?" Cassie asked, her throat scratching as she talked.

Nate pulled her close. "I'm no magician. I'm a monster, remember?"

"We have to get out of here now," Whitney said as she stood in the broken doorway. "Owen brought the cars around."

Nate stood, and Cassie tried to push herself up also.

"No, let me carry you," Nate told her.

"No thanks," Cassie replied.

Nate didn't let her stand all the way as he scooped her into his arms.

"If you walk out of here like you're all better, then they'll know I used my blood to heal you," Nate whispered into her ear.

"You did what?" Cassie didn't have the energy to make her accusation sound as mad as she was.

Nate pressed his lips to hers as he walked out of the diner carrying her to the waiting car. Gently, he put her down in the backseat before sliding in next to her.

"Should I head to your father's place?" Owen asked from the driver's seat.

"No, take her back to her uncle's. I'm sure they have the wards fixed and relocated," Nate replied. Owen nodded and took off.

"Are you going to explain—" Cassie began, but Nate put his hand over her mouth.

"I'll tell you later," he answered quietly.

Cassie pouted, but still had no energy to argue. Nate was getting off easy, but she wasn't going to let up until he clearly explained what he'd done.

Owen drove quicker than normal, and that was saying a lot since he rarely drove the speed limit as it was. Cassie caught his glances back to her in the rearview mirror. She was feeling better, but was still sore all over. Her magic was drained, making her spell and the weird tingling from Nate's magic almost gone.

"I think I need to sleep," Cassie muttered as her eyes began to droop.

"Don't," Nate told her. "You've lost too much blood. If you go to sleep, you might not wake up."

Cassie shrugged and kept her eyes closed. She had already made her peace with dying.

The windows opened beside her, and the cold wind whipped her in the face.

"Hey," she complained, "it's cold outside."

"Good," Nate replied.

Cracking open her eyes, she glared at him. He shrugged as Owen let out a sigh of relief; he was turning down her street to her house. Cassie didn't get a chance to get comfortable again as Owen pulled to a sharp stop in front of her house. Nate held her when she jerked forward.

The door was suddenly opened as her uncle reached in and easily pulled her from the car like she was a doll.

"She's injured," he growled.

"But alive," Nate replied. He neither backed down nor took Cassie from her uncle.

Uncle John carried Cassie back inside the house. They stopped in the living room, and he laid her on the couch. A coven elder Cassie had only seen once as a child was waiting for them. Taking on look at Cassie, the older woman gasped.

"She's close to death," the woman said to the men in the room.

Cassie finally noticed the room was filled with people.

Her uncle and Nate stood the closest to her, but also in the room were Nate's father, who was her uncle's best friend, and a couple more guys she didn't know the names of.

"We need to call Maria back," John told the room.

There were numerous coven members in the room also, and they all began to talk. The coven leader—a thin, pale woman that looked far from her prime—clapped her hands. Everyone fell silent.

"We won't be calling back Maria. Alexandria is more than capable of healing what's left to be healed, and the boy did the rest by applying our potions before bringing her back. She will live and be fine. More important is to find out how the wards were broken and how they got this far in town." The older lady looked at Nate's father as she spoke. He nodded. "Keep her on the first floor here with us, and you all figure out where they came from and where they're hiding in town."

The men in the room all bowed to the woman before they left.

"Except you, Nathaniel. You will stay here and finish what you started. She will need your blood for the potion."

John hesitated to leave with the men. The older lady tsked at him, and he looked back to Cassie. She gave him a meek smile with all the energy she had left.

The room grew quiet without the men in it.

"Look her over and see what we need to add to it. We need to replenish her blood so we can do the bond tonight," the coven leader spoke again.

Cassie's mouth dropped open. She still had a week before the ceremony. This wasn't how it was supposed to go.

Nate sat beside Cassie and looked into her face.

"No," Nate said to the lady.

"What?" she exclaimed as she turned to him.

Nate pulled Cassie protectively into his arms.

"The binding will be her choice. I won't force that on her," Nate stated. Cassie could feel his heartbeat pick up as he spoke. The old lady was small, but even Cassie knew the power within her was more than meets the eye. She was the leader, after all.

"That isn't your choice," the lady said as she moved forward. "Your father and I agree that it's too risky to wait. They know about her. They will try to take her again. For her safety and ours, we need to make her one of us. We have a forty-eight-hour window to get your blood in her to bind her once you drink hers. We need to do this now."

"I won't do that to her. She spent her whole life not knowing about this stuff because you guys were afraid she was one of them. Now that you know she isn't, you're forcing her to join us without any time to process all of this. I refuse to bind to her without her consent."

The older witch looked at him, measuring his words. With a nod, the witch turned to the first one she had addressed.

"Make the healing potion," she ordered the younger woman.

"Just know this: she will be your responsibility if she joins them instead. You will be the one that will have to hunt her down and kill her," the coven leader told Nate.

"I accept that, Priestess Carson," he replied, nodding to her.

The coven leader clapped her hands and the women that were all standing around watching the exchange hurried out of the room into the kitchen. Nate was left alone with Cassie. She didn't know who the lady was until Nate called her by name. She was the leader of the coven and had been since her mother died several years before.

"You promised to explain." She barely had the energy to sit, but she had plenty to listen to him.

"Which part?" Nate asked.

"First about me being your responsibility, and then about your magic healing abilities," Cassie replied as she leaned back on the couch.

Gracefully, Nate sat down and slid her over to his lap. Cassie couldn't help but snuggle into his arms; he was warm and safe.

"Remember how I told you there are several clans of night humans?"

Cassie nodded.

"Well, one of them hates skinwalkers. They've been trying for years to stop the clan from binding to witches. Back many years ago, the witchling that passed her apprentice exam would be given as much time as she wanted to find her mate. In that system, you would have had years to learn about us and what it all means, but we had to change when the other clan would come to take our witchlings before they could choose a mate. Remember, it's an eye for an eye with us. Everyone has to have a partner. When they took one of the witches, then that meant we would have a skinwalker without a mate. Now we bond within two weeks to keep the witchling and the skinwalker safe."

"My two weeks isn't up," Cassie pointed out.

"Yes, because of that they especially want you," Nate replied.

"Is that what all those extra protection details were for that I kept overhearing Whitney and Owen talking about?"

"Yes. We've had to be extra diligent with you. They know it won't just be crippling to our coven if they take my mate, but to the whole skinwalker clan in general. I might be able to find another mate if you're gone, but it won't be a perfect fit, like you and I are. They know that, and will do anything to keep you from bonding to me."

"That's why the coven wants to do it now?" Cassie asked.

"Yes. And by not doing it, we're giving them a chance to take you again."

"What happens if they take me?" Cassie really didn't want to know, but she needed to.

"They will enslave you to them. We've found the bodies

of the witchlings they have taken in the past. They drain all the magic from them and then turn them into night humans. By the time we find them, they are no longer the humans we knew, but monsters that only follow orders and crave blood."

"And it will be your job to hunt me down if they get me?" Cassie asked, horrified by the idea of being forced into that situation. It was bad enough they wanted to marry her off, but a life of being a monster that lived on blood sounded even worse.

"Yes. I'm putting everyone at risk by letting you not bind to me," Nate replied, stroking her hair as she lay against his chest.

"And your magic?" Cassie asked, changing the subject.

"I told you. I'm no magician. I don't do magic or magic tricks. What I did, any night human can do. I healed you with my blood," Nate explained quietly.

Closing her eyes, she nodded. She was out of energy again.

"What do you mean?" she asked.

"We don't get sick. Our blood is kind of like super healing. Night human blood can heal day humans. Just one drop was enough to get the wound on your leg to close. It took a bit more to get your insides to stop from shutting down."

"You gave me your blood?" Cassie asked, yawning. "Ewww."

Nate chuckled and made her head bounce as he did so.

"Only you would be less afraid of dying and monsters chasing you in the night, and more grossed out by sharing blood," Nate told her.

"Oh, they were gross, too," Cassie added, feeling her world fade as she drifted off to sleep. Nate's lips pressed to her forehead.

"Sleep, gorgeous. You will be all better soon."

Cassie woke on the couch in her uncle's house. It was perfectly quiet. She sat up and waited to hear something—anything. It was still silent. Slowly, she stood and walked to the front door. As she passed the front window, she looked outside at the street. There was a slight haze, and she knew what that meant—the coven had put up a protective spell all around the house. Cassie went to the front door and tried to open it. The handle didn't budge. No one was in the house because they had sealed it from the outside.

Hurrying, she ran to the back door in the kitchen and tried to open that. It would not budge either. They had locked her in. She was trapped.

She began to feel lightheaded and leaned against the counter to keep herself stable. Everything came back to her quickly. She had been sleeping. Someone had taken her. She ran from those half-transformed skinwalker monster things, and one ended up cutting her. Cassie pulled up her sleep pants. There wasn't a mark on her leg. Yes. That came back, too. Nate had used his blood to save her, and the coven tried to force him to bind to her. *He refused.* Cassie slid to the floor. *He actually refused.*

Cassie tapped her fingers on the tiled kitchen floor. There had to be something she could do. They made it very clear that none of them planned to summon her aunt even when she was dying from loss of blood. They were more willing to let her die than let Aunt Maria come back. That was the key. There was a way to join the coven without bonding to a skinwalker. But how was she supposed to do that without her aunt to help? She was sure there was nothing more in the library to look at. They didn't find a single thing to help in the books they had borrowed. Cassie tapped her fingers more. There had to be something.

The picture. That was something.

Rising, Cassie hurried upstairs quietly in case her uncle was home. She passed his bedroom door, which stood wide open. He wasn't home. She opened up her door and paused.

Sprawled across her bed was a familiar form with a dark hair. Cassie froze in her tracks. She didn't want to wake him.

Quietly, Cassie made her way from the door to her book bag. She slid her hand into the half-open back pocket and pulled out the picture just as quietly as she came in. All those years of practice being quiet were worth it. Cassie stood up and snuck out of her room. Cautiously, she walked into her uncle's room. She wasn't really allowed in there, but he wasn't home, and thus couldn't stop her.

Cassie pulled out the folded-up picture, certain she had seen it once before in one of the frames on her uncle's wall. She walked over to his bed and began looking at all the pictures. There were some from his childhood, and a large set of his parents. Nearby was one almost as large that was of her mother. Cassie stared into the eyes of the lady that she never met. She saw how much she looked like Maria, but Cassie knew what those eyes were saying—her mother felt just as trapped in the coven's secrets as Cassie now was. John had always said her mother was kidnapped while out with one of the coven travels, but Cassie had a feeling it was otherwise. Those eyes told her all she needed to know. She had to be sure the coven knew that she was in charge and not them. This *making her bind when she didn't want to* stuff was the first step of losing herself to the coven and all of its rules. Cassie had wanted, since she was little, to join and be part of the family she was never allowed to be around, but now she wasn't so sure. Maybe running away was a better choice.

A cough behind her told Cassie she wasn't alone in the room. She didn't need to turn around to know who it was. Nope, running away wasn't an option. Nate would be able to find her anywhere she went.

"Did they lock you in here with me, or did they give you a choice?" Cassie asked without turning toward him.

"I offered to stay. I knew you'd be pissed when you woke, and I didn't want you to be alone after last night,"

Nate explained.

Cassie paused at each picture, searching for the match to the one in her hand. There had to be at least sixty pictures on the wall. She smiled as she found her own face.

"What's going on up here?" Nate asked, close enough to gently touch Cassie's head.

"Last night, or rather this morning, isn't completely clear, but I do remember it. They were going to force me to bind to you without my permission," Cassie replied, still looking through the photos.

It was near the end and up high, but Cassie found the one she wanted. Cassie turned to find a chair to climb on, but Nate was already close enough. He reached up and took it down, handing it to her without being asked.

"Yes. They take the word of the seer seriously. She said you'd be the end of us if you didn't join us," Nate replied, watching Cassie as she turned the frame over and opened it.

"How could she know that? She had never touched me," Cassie replied. She had heard of the seer, but had never met her. There was no way the seer could have predicted Cassie's future without them actually meeting.

"She didn't meet you; she met your mother." Nate watched her intently.

"My mother was part of the coven," Cassie replied. At least that's what everyone told her.

"Yes, without a mate," Nate explained.

Cassie looked at him. *Then where did I come from?*

Nate saw her confusion. "You mother was added to the coven without a mate because it was predicted that her child would bring about the end to our ways," Nate answered. "She was never allowed to have a mate, and thus they thought they could stop the future from happening."

"But she had me," Cassie added.

"And that's why they easily agreed with John to keep you from the coven until it was proven you had night human blood in you. It was against skinwalker law for anyone to mate with your mother. Obviously, someone broke that law. So they're all worried that you will leave us and thus bring about the end to the coven," Nate explained. "What's with the picture?"

Cassie glanced down at her hands. She had stopped opening the frame, but refocused when Nate reminded her of the task. She began to unscrew the knobs holding the frame together. Gently, she set the frame on her uncle's bed and pulled off the back. The paper underneath kept the picture hidden, but she pulled that off, too. As soon as the paper was gone she knew this was the same picture. It had been bent back so that the full picture wasn't visible in the frame. Cassie pulled it out carefully, unfolded it, and laid it flat next to the one she held. It was identical.

"Who's that?" Nate asked, pointing to the fourth, previously hidden person from the framed picture.

"My uncle, I guess," Cassie replied, looking at the two photos.

Sure, it was easy to Photoshop something, but the framed picture had been hanging on her uncle's wall for as long as she could remember. It was even covered by years of dust. The guy who met her in the library was speaking the truth. She had an uncle; one no one had ever told her about.

"Where'd you get this picture?" Nate asked, pointing to the one she had brought in the room.

"Some guy gave it to me and told me he was my cousin. He said this was proof, and I took it without believing him." Looking closer at her unknown uncle, Cassie asked, "Who's this guy?"

She had always thought it was strange, how far apart in age Maria and John were because her mother and John were close, but now she could see. The mystery uncle was older than Maria, and another middle child.

"I've never seen him before, or even heard anyone talk about him," Nate admitted.

"But if he's one of my family, then he must be a

skinwalker, right?" Cassie replied.

Nate picked up the picture and stared at it.

"He had to be. Maybe he died or something," Nate suggested.

"Or maybe there are just more secrets that they don't want us to know," Cassie added. "How much does your dad share with you?"

Nate shrugged. "I'm not part of the clan yet as a full member, just as you're only a witchling. When you join the coven, then I get to join the clan. Until then, they let me keep track of all the people our age, but I don't attend meetings."

Cassie nodded. It seemed that Nate was beginning to feel a bit like her. He was busy thinking of everything as it had played out over the past few days. There had to be as much kept from him as from her since the coven and clan were quickly trying to get them to bind.

"What do you think is their problem? What are they keeping from us?" Cassie asked as she put the picture back. She didn't have to keep it out. She had her proof, and now all she needed was her uncle to ask about it.

"I don't know."

"John will tell me," Cassie said confidently, even though she wasn't completely sure he would. He had been nicer and more forthcoming, but even he couldn't tell her everything.

"No, he won't. I'm sure my father has forbidden it. All we can do is wait and see what they are up to at the meeting tonight."

That was one option Cassie hadn't thought of. She also didn't know Nate would easily join her side on everything. Nate Bay was full of surprises lately.

The moon was hidden by the clouds, but Cassie wasn't worried. For some strange reason, she trusted Nate completely. Granted, she still didn't want to be bonded to him; however, he wasn't her enemy in all of it. In fact, he was as much of an ally as Whitney was.

"You sure this will work?" Cassie asked. She had spent all afternoon making a counter-spell that would allow them to leave, and no one would know as long as they returned in two hours' time. In theory, the spell would do just that, but Cassie doubted that she could stand up to the strongest witches in the coven that had set the spell.

"I know it will work. Why do you think they're so set on binding you to me? Because you have power, and they're all afraid of you," Nate told her for the tenth time.

She didn't feel like she had power. Sure she had set the wards around her room, yet someone had come in and taken her right from her bed.

Cassie took the potion and put it in two cups, then gave one to Nate. It turned out that in offering to stay, he was as stuck as Cassie was in the house. The coven seemed to trust him about as much as they did her.

"Bottoms up," she said, clinking her glass to his. Nate grinned and downed the potion all in one gulp.

Cassie tipped up her glass and tried to do the same. It would take her more than one gulp, but she knew from previous experience all potions she made tasted horrible. She never got the knack of covering up the natural taste of the plants used.

Cassie sputtered, but kept the potion down.

"That wasn't bad," Nate told her. She had forewarned him of the taste.

"You've got to be kidding me. I could cook better meals at the age of five than how those taste."

Nate reached down and took the bag they were going to have to take with them. They needed more than just a spell to get out of the house. They would have to get past the skinwalkers and the coven to get to the meeting.

Leading the way outside, Nate took one step and sniffed the air.

"There's no one this direction." He pointed as he began

to walk into the dark of the night.

She paused before deciding to follow him. Her last nighttime excursion wasn't a pleasant memory. Turning to her as if he could sense her hesitation, Nate held out his hand and waited for her to take it. Cassie took a deep breath and ignored the fear that told her to go back inside. At his touch, everything faded away and was replaced by confidence. Cassie was sure it was his confidence, because it wasn't hers.

They walked a brisk pace through the backyards of her neighbors before turning toward town. It was going to be a ten-minute walk, but Nate kept the pace fast enough that they wouldn't need the ten minutes they had planned. As they paused in the last yard of the neighbors, Nate lifted his head again and sniffed the air. He pushed Cassie back in the yard and covered her with his body as he pressed her to a tree. Two young men came walking down the sidewalk. Cassie peeked from under Nate's arm. One of them seemed too distracted to notice them as they hid in the shadows, but the second paused mid-step to sniff the air just like Nate. He shook his head and continued with his friend down the path.

"There are a few people out," he explained quietly. "They're lower skinwalkers. Just follow my lead, and we can make it past them without a problem."

Cassie nodded as butterflies twirled in her stomach. He was so close that all she would have to do was tip her head back, and she could kiss him again. She hated that she felt that way, but she really wanted to feel his lips against hers again. Nate looked down, and his eyes glowed in the dim light. He seemed to feel the exact same way.

Nate took a deep breath and pulled back. "Ready?" he asked.

Cassie did not trust her voice and could only shake her head. Nate held her hand gently but firmly. He showed the way, sticking to the shadows of the buildings as they made their way down the street. When they arrived at city hall,

Nate ushered Cassie around back. He led the way by climbing up to a window he knew was left unlocked. He had explained beforehand that he used that entrance often because he was running late. Once inside, he showed Cassie the way through unlit corridors to a hiding spot above the stage. It took longer than normal because she had to continue to break the spells that had been cast to keep them out. By the time they made it to the stage, the auditorium was filled with the noise of people talking while they waited. Nate sat down first and made room for Cassie to nestle between his legs since the height of the latticework was much higher than she was comfortable with. Nate kept his arms around her waist even though she was tucked in tight enough not to fall.

The meeting was to start right after they were settled, and they had made it in time to not be detected. Below them on the closed stage stood Uncle John, Nate's father—Mikel, Harry Mala—Owen's father, and Charles Timber—Mikel's friend, and right-hand man.

"You know how I feel about that," Mikel scolded John.

"I don't care how you feel. Cassie is my responsibility. You can't just go and force her to mate with your son. Do you know what the coven will do with her?" John was upset, his hands shaking.

"Enough. I've told them that I approve of the mating. That's all there is to it." Mikel glared at John.

John paced around the stage and ground his hands together. Cassie knew that stance was to keep him from hitting the alpha of the clan.

"Can't you cut him some slack?" Harry spoke up. "You know what the clan did to Gabby and how they reacted to Maria. You can't blame him for keeping Cassie from them. You'd do the same if they had tortured your sisters."

Nate reached forward and covered Cassie's mouth as she gasped.

"They won't harm a hair on her head. I promise you that," Mikel replied. "My son genuinely cares about her. If they want us to continue supporting them, they will leave her alone." Mikel's eyes flashed the same blue color as his son.

"We need to get Maria home." John was finally able to control his anger. "She can stabilize both of them until they are ready to bond."

"Or change the bond if Cassie wants," Harry added. Mikel glared at him with his glowing blue eyes.

"Change, delay, I don't give a crap," John said, stepping between Mikel and Harry. "All I know is that if we leave the coven to perform the bond, you know they will strip her of her powers for the good of all. Who says it's for the good? Their good, or ours. I know that Gabby was never the same again. I'd rather die fighting them all than allow that to happen. We need to stop this."

John looked more than desperate.

"We can't stop them," Charles said so quietly that Cassie almost missed it.

"Becky is no match for Holly," Mikel added. Becky was Mikel's wife and Nate's mother. Cassie felt him tense as his father spoke of her. Holly was the head witch of the coven. "If Maria had just bonded to her mate, we wouldn't be in this predicament. You would have been at full power and able to stand up to them. As a half skinwalker, there's nothing you can do to stop them."

"That's why I came to you," John added. He stared at Mikel, silent words being passed between them.

"I can't stop it," Mikel replied. "It is what it is."

Cassie felt Nate's grip tighten at his father's words. It wasn't the first time she had heard him say that, but it had been a long time. Many times throughout their childhood he had told Nate those words, and it was never the outcome Nate wanted. With one swift and silent movement, Nate picked Cassie up and made it across the walkway over the stage. The curtain was being opened, but they didn't stay around—Nate was already taking them away. Cassie could almost feel the pain inside him as he raced out of the building.

"You have to run away from here," he said as he set her down outside.

Cassie was shocked by his words.

"If the coven is really going to strip your powers, I can't let you stay here," Nate told her, taking her hand and walking her back to her house.

"What if I said that cousin of mine offered to help me so that I don't have to bind to anyone on Friday?"

Nate paused. His beating heart, which was breaking in two at the thought of Cassie leaving, slowed.

"Then tell me how I can help you."

CHAPTER 10

Cassie nervously sat, waiting for Nate to finish his call with his father. He insisted that he be able to take Cassie to the library to study for school. It didn't sound like he was winning the argument, but when he returned with a smile, she was sure they would be able to leave the house without being tracked.

"You have one hour. I sure hope your cousin shows up by then," Nate told Cassie as he tucked his phone away.

"You hope? I hope, too. I'm the one they plan to drain and use as electricity to power the clan," Cassie replied.

She knew only a little about the coven binding powers, and she was more than scared of it. Only the head priestess could do it, and Cassie had a feeling Holly Carson would be more than willing and eager to do so since Nate had dumped her daughter Jess to be with Cassie. The draining of a witch was a serious crime, and one that was only allowed by the coven elders because they could do it without killing the witch. That didn't mean it was a pleasant experience. The only people she had heard of it happening to were people that broke sacred laws. And they were never good people to begin with, so no one cared too much when they were punished.

Cassie shuddered at the thought. If she didn't find her cousin, then she would have to run and never come back. She wasn't about to let the coven take away her magic. That was the only connection she had left to her parents. She might not have known either her mother or father, but in every spell she cast, her parents were watching over her.

"They're on their way here right now," Nate told Cassie, squatting in front of her so that they were eye-to-eye. "I won't let them do that to you. I promise you."

Cassie nodded. In reality, it wasn't like he could do much. He turned into an animal on the full moon and a monster on other nights. He wasn't part of the coven. Cassie was unsure that he could even help.

Nate stood and paced the room. He was anxious to get out of the house, but she was even more so. She had packed her school bag with books, but he had packed his with her stuff in case she needed to run, which was becoming more and more likely. Cassie watched him moved back and forth. He was human, yet she could still see the animal in him. He might have been on two legs, but she could easily picture him on four. His elegant pace made her a bit jealous.

It had been so long since she had seen the old Nate—years, in fact—but he was back, and it felt like nothing changed. All they needed was Owen, and the gang would be complete. Cassie missed those days. It felt close to being real again, but now it was anything but happy days.

"They won't let Whitney come with you because they're afraid she was the reason that they got you the first time. A female skinwalker can be hard to trust for most. Heck, anything outside of the status quo is hard for them," Nate explained.

Cassie nodded. Words were getting harder to say as her nerves grew while they waited.

She hadn't talked to Whitney since she had spent the night as a tiger with her. She wasn't there when Cassie woke and opened the window, but Cassie didn't blame her friend. If Whitney had somehow broken the wards of the room, it wasn't on purpose. She would never do that, no matter what everyone else thought.

Nate waited at the doorway as someone drove up to the house. A second car followed not too far behind.

Holly Carson stepped out of the second car with Mikel.

Cassie tried not to look at Nate as the high priestess and the alpha walked to the house. If she had set the spell around the house, then maybe Nate was more than correct. Cassie had broken the head priestess' spell. So what did that mean about Cassie's powers?

Nate stood at the door and waited as Mrs. Carson removed the magical barrier. Nate stepped back as his father entered with the lady that Cassie was beginning to see might have encouraged her daughter to put the spell on Cassie the week before. It was against coven law to do spells on others in the coven, but since the witchlings weren't full members, it was a gray area, and not many were punished. It was also hard to punish for a spell that Cassie counteracted by diminishing the spell signature.

"We expect you back here in one hour," Mikal told Nate. He nodded to his father.

"You are responsible for her. If she's taken or turned, you will have to deal with her," Mrs. Carson scolded Nate. He nodded to her, but he was finished respecting her just like Cassie was.

Nate held out his hand for Cassie. She took it as Nate pulled her to the door. He kept his arm on her like he was afraid they would tear her from him. Cassie figured that was what it would come down to unless she found a different solution.

"Oh, I have one question," Cassie said as she paused. Nate's eyes grew big. That wasn't part of the plan, but Cassie had to ask. She might not get the chance again.

"What were the seer's exact words when she read my mother's future?"

Nate relaxed since the question was one that didn't give away anything they were about to do.

If Holly was surprised that Cassie knew, she hid her shock. Instead, she placed a well-manicured fingernail on her chin, tapping it as if she had to think.

"She will be the end of the witches and skinwalkers as we

know it," Holly replied. "We are hoping the old seer was wrong. They tend to diminish in reading the future with age. But it has yet to be proven otherwise."

Holly raised an eyebrow in challenge. No, she wasn't a fan of Cassie, but she didn't care. The lady had decided she was going to bind Cassie to Nate without her permission, and take away her only link to the community through her magic. Cassie didn't need her as a friend.

Nate nodded to his father, pulling Cassie through the door and to the second car before she could say anything else.

"That was lucky," Cassie said as they both slid into the backseat.

"Lucky?" the driver asked, turning around. It was Owen.

Cassie jumped forward and gave him a hug from around the seat.

"You freaking scared the life out of me the other night," Owen scolded Cassie, flipping his hair out of his face as he began to back the car up. "You don't have permission to go getting yourself kidnapped or bleed half to death. What in the world were you doing? Do I need to lock you in a tower to keep you safe?"

"Oh. I forgot to ask your permission," Cassie replied, going along with him. She needed this; it felt much more normal with Owen teasing her. Like nothing had changed.

"Yes you do, young lady," Owen used his best parental voice.

"So did you volunteer, or were you told to chauffeur us to the library?" Nate asked, something hinted in his voice that Cassie should listen to their conversation.

"I'd have to volunteer to keep that one out of trouble, but I didn't know you were going until your father called," Owen replied, driving them on their way.

"With orders to keep an eye on us, I'm sure." Nate sounded like he was joking, but his hand squeezing Cassie said otherwise.

"Yeah, your father can be crazy protective of you

sometimes," Owen replied, not having the slightest clue what was going on.

Cassie turned to Nate as Owen continued to drive and tried to read his expression. He was watching Owen and the road at the same time, and had yet to let go of her hand. His nervous energy was enough to drive Cassie mad on a normal day, but now she wondered what it was all about. Owen was her best friend. If they told him the truth, she was sure he would be right beside them. In fact, she was more than sure he would be all for keeping the bond from happening.

"Where's Whitney?" Cassie finally asked.

Owen looked into the rearview mirror to Nate before replying.

"She couldn't make it. She said to tell you *hi,*" Owen lied. Cassie stared in disbelief at her friend. She was used to him telling jokes, having fun, and occasionally lying to Whitney, always about the clothing she was wearing, but Cassie had never been lied to.

Owen looked back to the road, refusing to make eye contact with Cassie. She was hurt. He was her best friend; how could he just lie to her? It almost seemed like he was throwing their friendship away. All the stuff with Nate had him upset, but they were friends. Cassie expected him to have her back, but again, Nate was correct. She needed to keep her mouth shut.

Cassie glanced at Nate, who was still looking ahead. He squeezed her hand again to tell her he knew she was there, but he didn't move an inch otherwise where Owen could see it. It was like he was waiting for something. Owen pulled up to the library and his mask of not caring wavered. He was grinding his teeth in anger. Nate didn't wait for Owen to turn off the car as he pushed his door open and pulled Cassie out. Owen hurried to shut off his vehicle and follow.

"We seem to have a babysitter," Nate said quietly to just Cassie. "The great coven leader suspects you might flee and that I might help you; she made Owen take an oath to watch over us. I'll have to keep Owen away for you to talk to your cousin. I don't know why your uncle and cousin aren't part of the coven, but if he can help, we need it."

"Yeah, and why my uncle had to give up his mate when my aunt didn't join. It makes me wonder about all of it," Cassie replied. Nate nodded. It was all a bit suspect at the moment.

"Where to today?" Owen asked as he finally caught up with them inside the library.

"I just have some studying to do and wanted to be here in case I need a reference book. You know how slow my uncle's internet can be, well it's close to non-existent with a magical barrier around the house," Cassie lied to Owen. He nodded in agreement.

She looked away like she was searching for a table to keep from staring at Owen too closely. He would easily be able to tell if she lied too much, so she had the excuse already ready for him, but if he asked more or looked closely, he would see something was up.

Nate pointed to the tables over by the window where Cassie first met her cousin, and she nodded to him like his choice was perfect. Cassie sat down and took out a book while Nate sat beside her and looked around. Owen stood at the window and watched them as they sat.

They sat in the library for about ten minutes with Cassie doing homework, until she knew her cousin had arrived. Cassie felt the magic in the air around her. She was sure her cousin was around somewhere. She grabbed a paper from her backpack and wrote down a random call number for a book several stacks away from where they were sitting.

"Can you get this for me?" Cassie asked Nate.

He nodded at his cue.

"Sure. Owen, can you come walk over this way with me? I have a few questions for you about the last meeting with my father," Nate told him. Owen looked taken aback by the request.

"I'll be right here," Cassie told him. "Not going anywhere."

Owen nodded and followed Nate to the row of books to find the one Cassie wrote down. Owen didn't walk down the aisle with Nate but stood and watched Cassie as she pretended to write more notes. Nate returned with the book and stepped in front of Owen as he spoke to him, breaking his view of Cassie.

"If you want to talk to me, now's your only chance," Cassie whispered to no one in particular, but she hoped that a certain someone would hear her.

"We can't stay here," Jack said as he grabbed her arm. His warm touch zinged with pent-up magic. Cassie looked up into his eyes, but he glanced away. "Your mate can only keep the other one away for so long. Your choice, come with me and learn how to stop all this nonsense, or stay here and be forced to mate against your wishes."

Cassie glanced at Nate's back. They knew it could come down to that. It wasn't like they hadn't talked about it. But now as the moment presented itself, Cassie was having second thoughts. Nate said he would protect her. She looked at his back and could tell Owen was about to move around him. She took Nate's backpack and stood up with her cousin. Nate had told her that if the moment came to leave, she was to leave. He didn't trust anyone in his clan or the coven now that he knew what they wanted to do with Cassie, not even Owen.

"Good choice," Jack replied, and in a blink they were outside the library.

"How did you ..." Cassie asked.

Jack shrugged. "I'm a witch. It's what we do."

Cassie laughed as Jack led her away, and the guys were left to search inside where they would never find her. Of course her male cousin was a witch. It wasn't like anyone in her family was normal after all. Yep, Jack was certainly part of the family.

Jack didn't use his transportation trick again since his car was only parked feet from where they ended up outside. He opened the doors to his black Ford truck and let Cassie inside. Soon enough they were on the road on their way out of town. Cassie was nervous to just run away, but it wasn't like she didn't plan to come back soon. All she needed was the key to getting out of the binding.

"You're a witch?" Cassie asked in disbelief even though she already had a demonstration of his powers.

It sounded so weird to say it out loud. She had never met a male witch before. She had heard about them, but that was just in books. In person, it was rare to come across one.

"Yes, just an apprentice, but I have a few spells perfected, like that one," Jack said proudly. "I take it you found the picture?"

"Yeah. Your father is my uncle," Cassie replied as Jack drove out of town. She shivered as they passed the diner where she thought she was going to die. It was way too soon to see that place and relive those memories. "So what do I need to do to get out of the mating?"

Jack laughed. "Straight to the point. Don't you want to ask more questions? Like how is it your male cousin is a witch?"

Cassie shrugged. "My best friend is a skinwalker."

"Yes, we all know Owen," Jack replied with a hint of malice.

Cassie found that odd; Owen never mentioned Jack, but she let it go. She was just going with Jack for answers. Now it looked like Owen owed her answers, too.

"No. My other best friend, Whitney," Cassie added.

Jack almost stepped on the brakes in shock. His mouth hung open, and he swerved into the other lane briefly.

"You mean a female skinwalker?"

"Yeah. She turns into a cat," Cassie replied. It was

strange; it was as if he had never heard of that before.

"You're serious?" Jack kept driving, but he was completely distracted by the conversation.

"Yes. I've seen her half shifted, and then fully shifted on the last full moon." Cassie watched Jack try to understand. He seemed completely shaken by her words. Was a female skinwalker that odd?

Jack kept silent, and Cassie didn't know if she could interrupt him. He was completely lost in his thoughts. It seemed he had driven the route they were taking many times, and he was on autopilot. Soon enough they were driving out of town. They didn't go far before he turned onto a country road, and then a dirt path that didn't even look like a road. Jack parked the car and got out. Cassie wasn't sure what to do. They were in the middle of the woods, and there was nowhere to go.

"Sorry about that," Jack said to her outside the car. He spoke words she couldn't hear, and the image of the woods around her faded. They were parked at an old farmhouse, complete with a big red barn.

Jack started to walk toward the old yellow house before turning back to her.

"I promise we don't bite," he teased.

Cassie stepped out of the car and followed him into the house.

"My dad is gone right now, but my friends are here. When I felt you enter the library, I kind of left them," he explained.

"But I just went to the library," Cassie observed.

Jack laughed. "You know my little travel trick? I can do it with one object, so I took my car over there in case you didn't want to see me, that way I could just head home."

"Hey, Jack, back so soon?" a sandy-blond-haired guy asked as they walked in the house.

"She must have turned you down again?" another guy added before they both saw Cassie.

The second guy quickly stood and wiped his hands on his pants.

"Sorry about that. We didn't think you'd actually come back with him." The chocolate-haired guy held out his hand for her. "Jared Colley," he introduced himself.

Cassie recognized him right away as the one who had been in the library before with Jack. His hand was warm as he shook hers. His brown eyes, which matched his hair, sparkled when she touched him. She had grown used to seeing too much in people over the years, so one of her reactions to meeting someone new was to channel her energy to tell if someone was a witch, born from a witch, or completely normal. Jared's energy was similar to skinwalker. He had to be a night human.

"Are you guys like another coven?" Cassie asked. She had never seen Jared or the other guy before.

Blondie chuckled. "Something like that."

Cassie had no clue what that meant, but she didn't want to stay around and explore her options. Something about the blond guy seemed off. Blondie had the same feeling as Jared, and Cassie knew he wasn't human, but he didn't come with the gentle, peaceful vibe of his dark-haired friend.

"So can we get this all done?" Cassie asked. She wasn't even sure they could help her.

"You want to break the oath of joining the coven via the bond between a skinwalker and witch, correct?" Jack asked, clarifying exactly what she was there for.

"Absolutely, that or getting a ticket out of here is my only option," Cassie replied.

Jack nodded. "My father said the coven wasn't to be trusted, but I never thought anyone else could see it. I'm glad he got out, and I know exactly how to get you out, too."

"Do we need to wait until he comes home to have help?" Cassie asked. She was eager to get away from the blond guy. His stares were now getting unnerving.

"Nope. We can do it right in the kitchen," Jack answered,

and his friends nodded.

Jack led the way from the well-furnished living room where the two guys had been sitting and playing video games, down the hallway lined with doors. Jack pulled the only open one shut as they neared it.

"You really don't need to see how a bunch of bachelors live," he commented.

Cassie glanced behind her to the guys following. Luckily, Jared was closer than the blond one. Blondie's eyes took in every aspect of Cassie and made her want to hide or take a bath, or maybe both.

They walked into the much larger kitchen, and Cassie had to guess that there was more than one room that went into making up the space. One side of the room looked like a normal kitchen with a stove, oven, fridge, and sink, but the other side of the room was more of an open area than anything else in the house. Large tables lined the wall and herbs were scattered all over.

"This is where I do my work," Jack explained, tapping one of the tables.

Cassie looked back at her cousin. At first glance, she assumed he was close to her age, but now as she looked closer she would guess he was older, just she didn't know how much older.

"I think you should have just about everything to make your potion," Jack told her.

Cassie looked at him for more of an explanation. 'Make your potion' sounded like she was a one-trick pony. She knew how to make many, and if that was what it took, then she wouldn't have come to him.

Blondie laughed at her confused expression. Cassie could feel anger at the stranger boiling inside of her. It wasn't like she got upset easily, but he was just throwing everything off.

Jack motioned to him, and his smile faded immediately.

"You need to make the same potion you did to pass your witchling exam," Jack explained.

"Oh," Cassie replied, not really sure what to make of what he was telling her.

Just a week ago, she would have eagerly agreed, but now knowing that her blood could bind her to someone else made her pause. Right now the only night human blood in her was Nate, and if she kept the potion away from him, it should keep her safe.

Sensing her confusion Jack continued, "Each witchling is assigned a potion to make. If you can make it, then you have advanced enough to move on to your mentor's care."

"That's not exactly what we were told. I was told everyone was given the same potion to make, and then we got to choose a mentor."

Blondie laughed again. This time both Jared and Jack glared him into silence.

"They're still doing things that way," Jared commented to the two guys with him.

"They don't like to tell you the part that you don't actually get a choice in all of it," Jack continued. "That's why I knew we needed to find you. You haven't grown up with all of them telling you their rules and making you into a sheep. You're one of the few who can see you are strong enough to make your own choices. That's why we need to help you get out of the binding. You're different than them."

"And how do we do that?" Cassie asked.

"By doing your spell, and then I'll make a counter spell to it," Jack explained. "If you do what they want, you do the spell and use it to bind to your mate. If I make the counterspell, then you are bonded to no one."

Cassie nodded. His logic seemed sound, but she was still unsure about using her own blood. Maybe she could do the spell without it.

"What is the spell they made you do?" Jack asked, swiping the table to clean it.

"A protection spell," Cassie replied.

Jared nodded. "That makes sense."

166

"Yeah. They'd need him protected," Blondie added.

Cassie looked at him. They seemed to know more than they were letting on. If they knew who her protection spell was for, then maybe they had answers the coven would never tell her. They were certainly the people she needed to be around.

"What do you need?" Jack asked, turning the conversation back to the task.

Cassie looked over the glass bottles and everything that was sitting out already on the table. Most of the stuff was there. At least enough to get started.

"This should be a good start. It takes about an hour to make, including brew times," Cassie explained. Jack nodded as he reached for a metal tray.

"Put everything you use here in the order you add it. I can make a counter-potion from that," he explained. Cassie nodded. "Then we shall leave you alone to do what you do."

Jack turned to his two friends and waved at them to go back the way they came. Cassie nodded to her cousin and reached for the comfrey and horehound to begin.

The guys left her alone, and it was time to focus on her spell. She needed to get out of the bonding—the sooner, the better. She had to hope her cousin was right.

Cassie tried her best to concentrate on the spell she was working on. She had made it work over a dozen times before asking to test, but she still needed her full attention to make it happen now. She really needed for it to work on the first try since she wasn't sure how many tries she would get before Nate showed up. While Cassie waited for the mixture to boil, she reached for her phone in Nate's pack. She turned it on and then realized she had no reception, which made sense since she hadn't even seen the place when they had arrived. Cassie tucked her phone back away and began to mix.

Her mind wandered as she began the repetitive motion of crushing and mixing, crushing and mixing. Would Nate come for her? He had to do what the clan asked of him, but she was sure that there was much now that he was questioning. Maybe Jack was right—had they raised Cassie with the full knowledge and acceptance of the coven, things might be different. It wasn't that way now. She questioned everything because she had never been a part of it. She had seen the other side of the coven, and now had seen even more. Not even a week ago all she wanted was to join the coven and fit in, but now she was also questioning that. What she really needed was Maria to come home.

Cassie reached for the bottle of Castilleja mollis leaves and found it empty. Glancing over at the second bench she found there were none there, either.

Cassie left the kitchen and made her way back to the living room. Instinct told her that she should be quiet. She slowed as she heard the guys talking.

"But what happens once they find out?" Jared was asking as Cassie stopped just out of view.

"Who cares if they find out? We'll have her as one of ours, and there will be nothing they can do," Blondie replied. Even his voice made Cassie cringe.

"My father will deal with the skinwalkers. Once we have Cassie bonded to everyone in our clan, there will be nothing the skinwalkers or the coven can do," Jack answered. "We will have her just like we planned."

Cassie's heart picked up. They were supposed to be helping her keep from having to bind to anyone. What was he talking about?

"Man. Stop teaming up on me," Blondie complained. They must have been playing games again.

"And you don't think she'll suspect anything?" Jared asked.

"Suspect? They've kept her in the dark about everything. She won't even know what we're doing when we combine her blood with the clan's. They should have raised her as a witch, and they would have been better off. They can't blame us for this one," Jack answered.

"How could they be that stupid?" Blondie asked. The video game they were playing continued to make noise as the guys talked. "Ha! Take that."

"They think she'll end the coven and the clan. Sure she will, by giving us her powers," Jack replied. The game beeped more and Blondie groaned.

Cassie leaned against the wall. This wasn't how it was supposed to happen.

"So that old seer is selling her out to keep their power?" Blondie laughed as the game music started back up.

"Oh, yes. What the urge for power will do to anyone. Cassie was never going to destroy the skinwalkers and coven. She was going to be the new seer, and the old one knows that. Why do you think they are eager to bind and drain her powers?" Jack replied. "The seer told the priestess, and they're in it together."

"We're not going to drain her," Jared replied, sounding concerned.

"No. But she won't be one of them much longer."

Blondie laughed, and Jack joined in. Cassie looked to the doorway she could see but knew it was no use. She was too far from home, and Jack being able to transport himself would stop anything she tried. She was trapped.

Part of her wanted to quit. All she had ever desired in life was crashing down around her, and everyone seemed to want something from her. No one cared about what she wanted. That was no one except for Nate. She might not want to be bonded to him, but he was her only chance.

Cassie silently made her way back to the kitchen. Using the knife she had been cutting the herbs with, she pierced her finger and rubbed a drop of blood on the necklace Nate had given her. Before they left her uncle's house, he had told her how it worked, and she sure hoped that the magical connection was intact even if her cell phone wasn't. Cassie wiped the blade clean and put her finger in her mouth as

Jared appeared in the doorway.

"Are you okay?" he asked, his deep brown eyes looking her over.

"I'm fine," Cassie replied with her finger still in her mouth.

Jared came over to her and pulled her finger from her mouth to inspect it.

"It was bleeding," he commented. His warm hand held hers. The bleeding had stopped, and there was only a mark left where she had cut it.

"What are you, part bloodhound?" Cassie replied, pulling her hand from his. She didn't want her blood near any of them.

"I've never heard a night human called that before, but I guess that would be an accurate description." Jared smiled, causing a dimple to appear on his left cheek. If she had met him in a situation where he wasn't conspiring to bind her to people she didn't want to be with, she might have called him cute. Whitney would have agreed.

"You're a skinwalker?" Cassie asked.

"No. I'm a night human, though, so I can smell blood better than a bloodhound," he replied, flashing her a smile again. She could slightly see the danger behind his smile. "Do you need help?"

"You do magic, also?" she replied, glancing at her half-done spell. Nate still hadn't shown up. Cassie was beginning to wonder if the magic around the house was blocking her signal to him.

"Not really, but I can mix and follow directions better than most, or at least better than the idiots out there."

Cassie nodded as she looked at the ingredients and got a good idea.

"Your offer is great, but I can't continue. I can't find the Castilleja mollis in here," Cassie said, pointing around the room.

Jack walked in right on cue.

"Castilleja mollis? Can you just use Castilleja levisecta instead? We have some that grows just about a mile away. Jared can go get it for you and bring it back in probably ten minutes," he suggested.

Cassie shook her head. "Nope, tried that when I first made the spell. I need mollis."

Jack shared a glance with Jared.

"I'm afraid we don't keep that one in stock. All our endangered plants are in very limited supply," Jack explained, his hands ruffling his familiar dark hair. His posture looked exactly like Uncle John as he did it.

"We grow it at the school," Cassie replied. They had a year-round greenhouse where they grew practically every endangered plant they used in spells. It was easier than getting permission each time, and flying to whatever remote location the plant grew.

"Then I guess we need to make a trip into town," Jared replied. Jack gave him another look, and Jared shrugged.

"Count me in," Blondie added from behind Jack. "It's been a few days since I've been in town."

Cassie looked at him. It wasn't what he said, but the way he said it. There was way too much going on inside that blond head of hair. The sooner Cassie could get away from him, the better. Every fiber in her body said to run as far away from him as she could. Blondie smiled at her as she shivered, like he enjoyed her discomfort. Jared moved in front of him and blocked her view.

"Then let's get going before it gets dark," he suggested.

Cassie hoped she was right, and the necklace would tell Nate to come to her. She hoped it worked as well as he described because this might be her only chance to get away from her cousin.

CHAPTER 11

Jack led the way around the school. It was closed for the day, and almost all of the lights were off. None of the few teachers left were witches or skinwalkers, so there was no help there. Cassie kept her pace slow as she looked around, like she was worried who was still there.

"Don't worry, the coven isn't here. I'd have smelled them," Jared told her as he took her elbow to pull her beside him. He threw his arm over her shoulder to comfort her.

Cassie nodded like that was her only concern. The coven was just one of her problems.

Jack went to the door that led to the greenhouse which was built on top of the school. He shook the handle and then looked back to his friends.

"I'll just take you in one at a time," he told them.

Cassie's eyes grew big. One at a time meant she would be left with Blondie at some point.

"Ryder," Jack said, pulling Blondie near the door.

In a flash, they appeared on the other side. Cassie considered bolting.

"He won't touch you this time," Jared said into her ear. His warm voice tickled her neck. "I'm here, and he wouldn't dare."

Cassie had no clue what that threat meant, but she didn't have time to think. Jack returned and grabbed her arm before she could protest, whisking her to the other side of the door and inside the school. Jack flashed back to the outside.

Blondie took his chance and stepped closer to Cassie. She took a step back, and he grinned.

"I've always liked my witches with a little fear in them. They taste much better that way," he said, his eyes flashing red.

Cassie would have just about had a heart attack if Jared hadn't made a perfectly-timed appearance, already in full swing at Ryder. His fist only connected with Ryder for a moment before Jack stopped him from continuing.

"Ryder, tone it down," Jack ordered.

Ryder just smiled at Jared.

"Sorry about that jerk," Jared apologized to Cassie. She didn't trust any of the three guys, but Ryder just made it on to her avoid-at-all-costs list.

"How do we get up to the greenhouse without setting off the charms?" Jack asked.

"We need the key from Mrs. Anton's office," Cassie replied. "If the doors are unlocked the normal way, the spells are inactivated."

Jack flashed away, leaving Cassie with Jared glaring at Ryder. Jack came back with a ring of keys jingling on his finger. Cassie nodded and led the way upstairs. Breaking into the school was weird, but it wasn't like she owed the coven anything. They were almost as bad as Jack and his scary friends.

Cassie waited at the door to the greenhouse while Jack tried each key one by one. Finally, he got the door open, but he paused. He turned to Ryder first.

"They're yours to take care of," he told him. Ryder gave his sinister grin and took off down the stairs back the way they came.

"We have some company, so pick it fast," Jack told Cassie.

Cassie weaved through the rows of plants and to the back where they had a full garden. Castilleja mollis grew best on the ground with other plants in the same family. Cassie knelt as shouting grew outside the door, and pushed through the plants to find the right one. Jack stood guard behind her as she did so.

"Got it," Cassie said, taking just enough to finish her spell.

Jared offered her his hand to stand and Cassie took it. Grabbing the leaves, Jack shoved them in his coat.

"Time to leave," he said as the door burst open.

Cassie's heart skipped a beat as the room grew dusty and all she saw were large clawed hands hanging at the side of the person who'd just entered.

"I'd advise you to take your hands off my mate," Nate growled.

Cassie looked down and noticed Jared was still holding her hand from helping her stand.

"*Your mate?* Seems you can't keep track of her, so maybe she isn't yours after all," Jared replied smugly.

"I found her here," Nate replied as he silently stalked closer, just as quietly as he had in the barn.

Jared tightened his grip on Cassie's hand.

"Where we come from, we don't mate without consent. Did you ever explain to Cassie what you were getting her into when you marked her?" Jared asked. His voice was steady, but he sounded upset.

Having no clue why he cared so much, Cassie stared at him. They planned to do the same to her, but in a much more permanent way.

"Cassie, I'd advise you to step back. This won't be pretty when I get done, and I don't want to get you dirty," Nate told her. The blue flashed in his eyes.

"Two on one and you're worried about her getting dirty?" Jared taunted. "If I were you I'd worry about yourself."

"I'm not worried about that, even if it was two against one, but I didn't come here alone," Nate replied.

Nate best friends, Nic, Jones, and Owen entered the greenhouse behind him. Owen dropped the severely beat-up body of Ryder on the ground. None of them were partially transformed, but they looked menacing nonetheless.

"If you wanted to give us more of a challenge, you could send someone else besides this one," Owen complained, kicking Ryder and causing him to moan. "But then again, any time I get to beat on him is a fine time for me."

Jack looked around the room before nodding to Cassie. She had no clue what that meant, but she didn't want to go back with him. There was no way to tell him without giving away what she overheard.

Jared nodded to Jack and dropped Cassie's arm.

"I'll be back to rescue you later, princess," he teased, just before Jack grabbed him and disappeared.

Nate didn't even hesitate, just lunged forward and grabbed Cassie. She already knew Jack couldn't take two people at once, so she was more than grateful to hold onto him. Jack flashed back in to grab Ryder before anyone could stop him.

Nate stepped back and cupped Cassie's face. He checked her over quickly, and then looked into her eyes. She could feel the worry pour off him, but she just smiled.

"Guess it does work." She leaned her forehead into Nate's chest.

Nate gave a sigh of relief and pulled her close into a hug.

"No answers?" he asked.

"They planned to bind me to their whole clan. They thought they could trick me into it," Cassie complained. Owen gave a grunt of disgust at the suggestion.

"Let's get you home," Nate told her as he put his arm around her to lead her away.

Nate and Cassie passed the guys as they waited, still on alert. Cassie looked back to ask Owen a question when she noticed him cover Nate's mouth with a cloth. Before she could protest, Nic did the same to her. She tried not to take a breath, but it was futile. Her world dimmed.

Cassie's sense of sight was the last to clear when she

finally regained all her senses. Nate was beside her, holding onto her. She could feel his touch and hear his breathing as he worried.

"Let your eyes adjust," he told her.

The room slowly came into focus. It was dimly lit, but Cassie had no clue where they were. The walls were lined with shelves that held supplies from everything like paper towels to floor polish—more of a closet than a room.

"Why did he—" Cassie meant to ask more but finally realized a few things she didn't notice the first time. Nate was topless, and she was handcuffed to him. Cassie quickly looked down and was relieved to find she wasn't topless like he was.

Nate laughed. Cassie shook her head. How could he laugh in a situation like this?

"Okay, let's start with: why are you topless?" Cassie asked, glad the dim room hid her blush. It wasn't as if she didn't like looking at him without a shirt, but she was baffled as to why he'd be that way.

"They need to display the mating mark on me before they bind us," Nate replied.

"What?" Cassie asked in shock. Nothing made sense.

"From what I can tell, they ordered Owen and Nic to save you and then take us." Nate touched Cassie's face, still looking her over as if he were worried she might be hurt. "What did your cousin do to you? When I finally felt your message to come, I was scared of what I'd find. You felt terrified."

"First let's get straight about the whole topless thing, and whether I should be worried that they'll be back to remove my shirt," Cassie added.

She didn't know how he knew how scared she was and wanted him to think she was stronger than that. She was still confused as to why they were in some sort of storage closet and used that as a distraction to her feelings.

"I can hear them every now and then. They're at least two

rooms over that way." Nate motioned to the left wall with his free left hand. "And, no, they already pulled your hair up, and if they hadn't knocked me out, I'd have killed them both for touching you. There's kind of an unspoken rule about touching another's mate."

"Hair up? Remember, girl who was told nothing." Cassie pointed to herself.

Nate smiled.

"To do the bonding ceremony they have to show that we both carry the same mark, our mark. Yours is on your neck and mine my back," Nate explained. He turned slightly for Cassie to see his elaborately marked-up back.

"Wow, when did you get that done?"

Cassie had seen Nate shirtless more than a few times since he played on all the sports teams and was constantly running around the school and gym with the jocks, but she had never seen a tattoo on him, and she would have noticed one as big as that one. The marking spanned his entire back, even wrapping around his rib cage and peeking out the front along with lines that streaked down past his elbows.

"The same time you got yours."

"Wait, you mean I get a mark a couple inches that only skinwalkers can see, and you get a full-body tattoo?"

Nate nodded. Cassie really didn't know what to think of that.

"It's not normally this large. The size that appears has to do with the people bonding together," Nate explained. "I wish I had been awake when the guys took my shirt. Maybe I would have been able to talk them out of being idiots."

"So this is bigger than usual?" Cassie touched the lines with her free hand. They were a dark color, but the dim light didn't let her see them completely.

"No. Let's put it this way. My father is the alpha of the clans, and his is about the size of a plate," Nate explained, holding out his free hand to show the size.

Nate's was more than double, or even triple that. Cassie

thought it was bad that everyone who saw her neck knew she was with Nate, but his was even more definite.

"I'm sorry …" Cassie didn't know what else to say.

Nate laughed again.

"Sorry? Why? This more than proves my status in the clan. No one can dispute it now," Nate replied. He didn't seem to care at all.

"So the markings have to do with the bond?" Cassie asked, mulling over her cousin and his blond friend, Ryder.

"Yes. It's an indication of your strength and mine together," Nate answered, unsure where the question was leading.

"So if I overheard my cousin mention that I was the next seer for the coven, and hence the reason they're trying to take my powers, would that have something to do with it?" Cassie asked.

Nate's eyes grew bigger and then he let out a hearty laugh.

"Glad this can amuse you," Cassie replied sourly, not understanding his delight. The coven was going to drain her power as soon as they did the bonding.

"Man, this makes much more sense now. When we were kids, I always wondered how you knew stuff you shouldn't know. Before I could ask you about it, my father forbade me from being your friend." Nate shook his head as he took it all in.

"Do skinwalkers that bind the seer get those markings?" Cassie asked.

"I wouldn't know. They don't let the seer have a mate," Nate replied. "Never in the history of the skinwalkers has the seer ever had a mate. Well, they were right about one thing—this is going to change everything."

Cassie couldn't tell if that was a good or bad thing. Her mysterious powers seemed to attract everyone. But it wouldn't matter much longer. She would be useless if they wanted to take them from her. She had no way to fight back.

"Why did your cousin bring you here?" Nate asked, changing the subject.

"He was having me make the spell I made to pass the exam again. He didn't have Castilleja mollis, so we had to break into the school to get it," Cassie explained.

"What did you learn from your cousin about stopping the binding?"

"That they want to bind me to their whole clan instead of one person. They didn't want to help me," Cassie explained. "I'm not sure there's even a way to keep from binding to join the coven."

"Umm, I brought you guys a friend, but now see maybe that wasn't the best idea," Whitney said from the open door behind Cassie. Jack was standing beside her friend.

Jack shrugged.

"The jig is up I guess." He lunged for Cassie, but Nate stepped between them just in time. Jack touched Nate and together they disappeared.

Whitney looked in horror at the scene. Nate was there one minute, and gone the next. Cassie stared at the dangling handcuff. If she had been holding Nate's hand, Jack would have never been able to take him away.

"We have to get to him now," Cassie told her friend.

"He just disappeared," Whitney added in shock, still staring at where Nate was just standing.

"Yes. My cousin is a witch—warlock—whatever you want to call him. And he isn't someone I want to leave Nate with," Cassie added, fearing for Nate's safety. Ryder was unstable, but she didn't know who else was now with Jack and his friends.

"A male witch? Impossible," Whitney said, still in shock.

Reaching up to her taller friend's face, Cassie put a cold hand on each cheek and looked straight into Whitney's eyes. "They took Nate. We need to go now and get him back."

Whitney blinked twice, coming out of her shock.

"He took Nate," she repeated as she came back to the

situation at hand. "Then good thing I brought these with me."

Whitney handed Cassie some invisibility potions they had made the summer before to sneak past her uncle. They had taken weeks to make, but they had perfected it by the end of summer when they had nowhere to go.

Cassie grinned.

"If this can fool one skinwalker, I sure hope it can fool the rest," Cassie added, dabbing the liquid on her face and arms. Whitney did the same and reached back to take Cassie's hand. The potion made them invisible, but not ethereal. They still needed to make it out of wherever Cassie had been imprisoned.

"We're in the school. They plan to hold the ceremony here at midnight," Whitney explained. "There are guards outside the room, and more patrolling the halls and the school grounds. We need to make it to the tree line before I can partially transform without anyone knowing, and can take you anywhere you need to go."

Cassie nodded her invisible head. It was time to go get Nate back. She didn't really want to go back to her cousin, but she couldn't leave Nate there. He might be able to get out of it himself, but she got the distinct feeling Nate was as much as prize as Cassie was.

CHAPTER 12

Whitney was right. Skinwalkers were everywhere, and it wasn't just the students from the school. There were adults wandering around also patrolling the area. When they made it to the tree line, Cassie didn't feel safe enough to break the spell, so they continued to walk farther into the woods. It cost them time, and Cassie wasn't sure how Nate was faring with her cousin and his friends. It didn't matter, though; if they didn't get away successfully, then they couldn't help him at all.

Whitney finally stopped. She mumbled the counter spell, and it worked on her first try. She was always better at magic under pressure.

"Time to get going. Where do we find this wonderful cousin of yours?" she asked.

Cassie shook her head. "I wouldn't describe him as wonderful."

"Ahh, come on. Ryder is Owen's cousin, so yours can't be any worse," Whitney added. "And a male witch. Why did he have to be on the bad side?" Whitney pouted.

"Bad side?" Cassie asked. She got the feeling Jack and his friends weren't good people, but the way Whitney said it made it all sound like a superhero comic.

"Yeah. Ryder is a wendigo," Whitney replied.

"Wendigo?"

Whitney just shook her head. "Guess loverboy didn't cover that topic yet. I don't know how you're keeping it all together without knowing anything. When we get time, we have to sit down and go over all of this. They should have never left you in the dark," she added. "Now on to finding your mate."

Whitney's eyes turned a brilliant green color, and her body seemed to gain a bit of mass. Cassie jumped a little at the change. She wasn't exactly used to the partial skinwalker form and had a feeling she would never be.

"Sorry. Partial transformation will help us here. Once you tell me where to go, in this form I can get us there faster than a car," Whitney explained.

"Head out past Miller's Diner. About half a mile farther is a path big enough for a truck, but it doesn't look like a road. The house is right there, so we should stop on the road out of town. By the way, that's cool that your eyes can change so many colors," Cassie added as her friend bent over and motioned for her to hop on, piggyback-style. Cassie would have laughed if they had time to sit around thinking about what they were about to do. It had to have been at least eight or more years since Cassie had a piggyback ride.

"Change color?" Whitney asked as Cassie climbed on her larger friend's back. It was a good thing that even partially transformed Whitney was more than six inches taller than Cassie; otherwise it would have been a bit awkward.

"Yeah. Normally your eyes are a steel blue-gray color, and then they turn green for a partial transformation, and then electric blue when you're a tiger," Cassie explained.

"I'm not a tiger," Whitney replied, and gripped her legs. "Hold on tight."

Cassie couldn't get another word out as she was forced to squeeze her eyes shut from the wind whipping in her face. She had never been on a motorcycle before, but she got the feeling that it was close to the same experience as getting a piggyback ride from her almost-monster friend.

She didn't have time to process what she had just heard from Whitney before they were standing on the road, facing the pathway to the house where Jack had brought Cassie.

"I'll scout ahead. I'm pretty quick, so I'll be right back,"

Whitney told her before Cassie could stop her.

Moments turned to minutes. Cassie waited, but Whitney didn't come right back. A feeling of dread settled over her. It took less time to go from the school to the other side of town than it would to reach the house. Whitney still wasn't back. Cassie peered down the pathway. It looked like a well-walked path, but not a driveway. She knew that was deceptive. There was a house and a barn back that way.

Cassie took a deep breath and began walking down the path. Whitney wasn't coming back. Cassie could feel it in her bones. She was only halfway there when her cousin appeared before her.

"So nice of you to join us, lovely cousin," Jack said.

Cassie stopped and stared at him.

"Where's Whitney?" she asked.

"Your lovely female accomplice who was, uninvitedly, snooping around my house?"

"Where is she?"

Jack shrugged. "Guess you should come with me to find out."

It wasn't like Cassie had any other option. He turned and didn't bother to look back to see if she was coming. Cassie followed behind him at a distance, keeping her eyes and ears alert. She hoped Whitney would just appear, even if she knew it wasn't going to happen. With a flick of his hand, Jack dissolved the illusion of the forest and led Cassie toward the large barn instead of the house. Cassie paused at the door as he casually entered.

"Not interested in seeing everyone again?" Jack asked from inside. "I promise my friends look scarier than they really are."

Cassie stepped inside the doorway and froze.

The red-eyed monster she had seen twice now was standing against the far wall. He licked his lips as he paced the length of the barn.

"And of course, you recognize your friends," Jack waved

his hands at Whitney, who wasn't moving on a table.

Nate was locked in a cage and pacing back and forth in it just like an animal, not saying anything. Nate stopped to give Jack an especially ugly glare from the cage. He wasn't touching the bars, but anger boiled in his eyes like he wanted to go all crazy-like and break out.

"I'd like to first explain that it wasn't my intention to hurt your friend there. She's the one that tried to jump me. All I was doing was defending myself," Jack said as Nate spoke at the same time.

"Cassie, get out of here. He's lying to you."

Jack waved his hand, and the red-eyed monster stalked near the cage. Nate kept perfectly still and glared at it.

"Ryder, you know the deal," Jack called to the monster as it slowly stuck an arm between the bars.

Nate jumped aside quickly and slammed the monster's arm against the metal bars. Ryder gave a loud shriek before swinging his sizzling arm around to attack Nate.

"Stop," Jared said as he stepped from the shadows. Ryder froze in his place.

"As I was saying," Jack continued, like his friends weren't in a staring battle behind him. "Your friend there's suffering from silver poisoning. What she needs you to do is to finish the spell you were creating when we left the house. Your protection spell will keep the silver from harming her."

"Silver poisoning? Like werewolves in the movies?" Cassie asked. She really needed a textbook on skinwalkers. Nothing made sense to her, and every time she turned around they were throwing more rules into it.

"Partially transformed skinwalkers are susceptible to silver just like the movies. That's the reason they bind to a witch. That makes it so they can fully transform even without the moon and don't have to go through the phases of partial transformation," Jack explained.

"Then she just has to transform?" Cassie questioned.

"But they can't without a mate, and, unfortunately, your

friend there doesn't have a mate. Hence the reason you need to finish your spell."

"I already have a mate. As far as I've been told, I can't change that. What good is my mating spell to her?" Cassie asked.

Was Jack asking her to choose Whitney as her mate? She was her best friend, and Cassie was willing to do just about anything for her, but that didn't sound like it was what Jack was saying.

"It isn't a mating spell. Yours is truly a protection spell, and if I'm correct, it's to protect against silver poisoning. No witch has ever been able to make that spell; that's why they assigned it to you."

"It's just a normal protection spell, I promise. I used it on myself. It kept me from getting cut," Cassie explained.

Jack shrugged. "Humor me."

Cassie looked at her friend. She didn't seem like she was in pain, but the lack of consciousness was a bit concerning.

"Cassie, don't do it," Nate said to her, breaking her stare at her friend. "He just wants to use your spell to bind you to them. Even after you make it, he won't let you use it on her. He's going to make you barter to get her safe. Let us die. Don't agree to what he wants."

Jack smiled, and now she saw that her cousin was more similar to Ryder than she first thought.

"Is that true?" Cassie asked.

Jack shrugged. "Maybe, but you won't find out unless you try. I can tell you one-hundred-percent that she will die if you don't try."

Cassie glanced at Nate. He was still staying away from the bars that burned Ryder, but his eyes were pleading with her. She returned her gaze to her friend. Whitney was the only light in the messed-up witch world Cassie was part of. She couldn't just let her die.

"Fine. Bring me the stuff I was working on, and I'll finish it," Cassie said.

"Come this way." Jack motioned for her to follow.

Cassie cast one last glance back at Nate. She tried her best to get to him understand she was sorry with her eyes. She didn't know what would happen next, but she had to try. Whitney was her best friend, and if her spell could save her, then there was no choice.

"I don't have to work out there?" Cassie asked, kind of wanting to stay with her friends and keep track of them.

"Of course not. That's where we keep the animals," Jack replied. He opened the kitchen door. Everything was right where she left it.

Cassie walked to the table where she had been working. Jack nodded to her and turned to leave.

"Wait. I need the Castilleja mollis," Cassie told him.

Jack laughed. "I guess Jared wins that bet." He went to the cupboard and tossed the leaves she had picked earlier onto the table.

"What bet?"

"Ryder bet Jared you used that as an excuse to leave. Jared said you really needed it. Twins can never seem to agree," Jack added before walking away.

Cassie looked down at the table. She didn't have many options. Jack was leaving her alone. It was time to decide what to do and Cassie didn't like her options. There was a chance she could get away. She could run back to town to get help, but she wasn't as fast as Whitney. By the time she got there, they were sure to have done something to Nate, Whitney, or both. What else could she do? She had to make the potion.

Cassie put the lid on the jar. Several wads of leaves were in the bottom of the jar due to lack of time, but Cassie didn't want to waste more of the precious time that her friends were locked up and suffering through. The potion was mainly done except for the last ingredient—that was the one part she couldn't do. They would need her blood to bond her to anyone, and giving it away easily made her feel like she was giving up. She hoped the spell would work without her blood, at least for Whitney's sake. And if needed, she could add a little blood before giving it to her, maybe.

Cassie sat down in exhaustion and stared at the vial. This was it. Her life was going to change in an instant, no matter what happened.

"Finished?" Jared asked as he came in the room.

"I hope," Cassie replied.

"I'm sorry it's turning out like this," Jared offered an apology

"Sorry?" Cassie was a mixture of confusion and a bit of upset as she replied. Sorry didn't cover the situation she was in, but it was also strange to be getting it from him.

"If I was in charge, it wouldn't be handled this way," Jared explained. "If you had just taken your test in a year or two, I might have been able to take over by then." Jared seemed genuinely disappointed.

"Take over?"

"Right now my father hasn't decided if Ryder or I will be next in line to be alpha. If I knew this was going to happen to you, I would have made my case to be in charge of what is happening. Now, I don't get a say." Jared was more than disappointed; he was upset.

Cassie was surprised.

"But you don't even know me," Cassie added. Why was a stranger that concerned for her?

"I don't?" Jared replied, raising an eyebrow. "Your favorite color is green."

Cassie shrugged. "Everyone knows that, or you could have guessed." Cassie currently had a green tank top on under her shirt. She almost always wore something green.

"You like chocolate," he added.

"Doesn't everyone?" Cassie was still unconvinced.

"But only with peanut butter and not mint," he continued.

He was getting more specific, but that still didn't mean anything. Any witch could get those details about someone, and he was friends with her cousin who practiced magic.

"When you look out a window, you long to be outside instead of trapped indoors. You wonder if it's possible to just run away and live in the woods. You yearn to be around nature," Jared continued.

This time, he was specific and scarily right. No one knew that about Cassie. She had never told another soul that she wanted to live outside in the trees. People already thought she was nuts as it was; she didn't need to add more fuel to the fire. Cassie stared at Jared. He gave a meek smile back.

"I know a lot about you, Cassandra Booth. Maybe even more about you than you know, but I didn't act quickly enough. Even you can still surprise someone I guess." Jared shrugged. "Ready to go get this over with?"

Cassie nodded, still confused as to why Jared knew things about her. Cassie moved to follow him, but he paused suddenly at the door. He turned just as quickly, and she was standing in his arms as they wrapped around her to keep her from falling and spilling her potion.

"The bond only works if you want it to," Jared said quietly. "Remember that." He tucked a loose strand of hair behind her ear.

Cassie looked up into his chocolate brown eyes and got a glimpse of his past. He was the good child. He did everything his parents wanted of him. Ryder was not. He used every chance he got to do as he pleased, and tried to get Jared blamed for all of it. His parents saw which child was the better one, but Ryder was strong and ruthless. Their father liked those qualities, and told Jared that until he could be that way he couldn't take over the clan. Jared was right. Anytime he wanted, he could call the clan his own. He could have stopped everything that was going on if he were in charge.

Jared broke his gaze from her. He was telling the truth,

no matter how strange that was coming from a guy who had helped take her and her friends hostage.

Jared spun and opened the door in one motion, then led the way back to the barn. Cassie squinted into the darkness as they entered. Nate was no longer locked away in a cage. He was now standing in the open, chained to the ground with a collar around him that seemed to be burning into his neck; it sizzled on contact with his skin. He didn't flinch or show any pain.

Cassie wanted to go over and rip the chains right off him. They were treating him like an animal. Cassie saw the skin around his neck bubbling with blisters. Nate didn't look away.

"Here's your potion," Cassie said, dropping the bottle to the ground but not hard enough to break it. "Now let my friends go."

Jack smiled from his seat near Whitney.

"While that would be a great deal, I can't just take some unknown potion from you and expect you didn't do something to poison us," Jack replied.

Cassie's eyes widened at the suggestion. She had never thought to do that, because he said it would cure Whitney. Did he expect her to just let her friend die?

"I wouldn't do that," Cassie replied, staring hard at her cousin. Ryder wasn't the only one that was ruthless.

"Well, cousin, I'm not one to just take your word. Show us that the potion works on your soon-to-be-former mate, and then I'll let you use it on your friend," Jack replied, hopping up and sitting on the table where Whitney was lying.

Cassie looked to Nate. If she wanted to really prove it was working, she would have to add her blood to it. Without her blood, there was a good chance it wouldn't work and then she couldn't use it on Whitney. If she added her blood, then she would complete the binding to Nate. Cassie glanced back at her passed-out friend. She owed it to Whitney.

She put her reservations away and turned to Nate. He watched her cautiously, like he knew something was going on. Cassie walked over to him and stood close.

"Did you poison it like he says?" Nate asked quietly.

"No," Cassie replied. "I wouldn't have even tried that. He said it could save Whitney."

Nate nodded. "I figured that much, but what—"

"I didn't have time to distil it like I'd like, so it works best if I make it into a paste by chewing it." Cassie took a wad of the leaves and put them into her mouth. They tasted absolutely terrible, but she didn't have any other options. She needed to get the potion in Nate with her blood to prove it worked.

"Promise not to make more out of this than I intend," Cassie asked him.

"What?" Nate asked in reply as Cassie reached up and gently pulled Nate's head down close enough that she could kiss him.

Cassie rubbed her front teeth over her lip that was still healing from the night before. Her blood was added to the horrible tasting potion through the crack. Nate was watching her lips as she chewed and pulled his head closer. For a split second, she saw him recognize what she was doing, but he made no motion to stop her. Cassie pressed her lips to Nate's and transferred the mashed up potion, now containing her blood that made it completely active, to his mouth.

Cassie pulled back and sucked on her lip to keep the blood from showing. Nate stood back up but kept his hands on her waist.

"You can spit out the leaves," Cassie explained. "It's just the juices you need."

Nate continued to chew and smiled as he did so. It didn't take more than a minute, and his wounds were completely gone. He swallowed the leaves and smiled at her. Cassie stepped back, breaking Nate's grip, but he was still watching her.

"See, works, now let me use it on Whitney," Cassie begged.

Jack grinned, and he hopped down from the table.

"I didn't think it would really work. You found a way." Jack was rubbing his hands in joy.

"Whitney now," Cassie said, bringing the conversation back to his part of the deal.

"Yeah, yeah," Jack replied, circling Nate and looking at the wounds that were now gone.

Cassie moved to go to her friend.

"No. You don't get to heal her. She's a skinwalker. One less won't hurt us. We need to bind you to the clan right now," Jack replied. "Ryder, get rid of the other girl. Jared, go call your father to tell him we need to do this now."

Ryder stalked over to Whitney.

Cassie moved to run over to her friend, but Jack flashed before her, and pulled her into the cage Nate was in before.

"Second thought. The girl isn't going anywhere. Ryder, go help your brother bring the clan here. This is exciting." Jack clapped his hands like he just won the greatest prize.

"But you said I could cure her," Cassie added as she grabbed the bars. They were solid silver-coated steel. Cassie wasn't going anywhere.

Jack shrugged. "I changed my mind." He waved at Jared and Ryder to go. They both left the barn in a hurry.

"You said," Cassie pleaded for the second time.

"I lied," Jack replied, smiling at her from the other side of the cage. He bent down and picked up the leftover potion. "It's going to take a lot more of this to protect the whole clan, but that's fine. Once you're bound to us, you can't refuse. This is great. I'll be the head of the clan in no time. I'll be the first witch alpha."

Jack moved to the doorway of the barn and looked out at the house.

"I'll be right back." He grinned as he left them. Cassie was locked away, Whitney was unconscious, and Nate was chained up.

The barn door slammed shut from the wind outside. It was getting dark out, and they would all be changing soon. She didn't have any options left.

'Change me,' Nate's voice said to Cassie.

"What?" Cassie asked.

'Change me,' Nate said again. This time, Cassie was looking at his mouth. It hadn't moved, yet it was him. She had no idea how she heard him, but it sounded just like him.

'You are my mate now. This is part of the deal. We can speak to each other in our minds, and best we do since otherwise they'll hear us talking,' Nate quickly explained. *'Now change me.'*

Cassie squinted her eyes at him. Nope. His mouth still wasn't moving. Yet she had no clue what he was talking about. Across the room, Nate huffed.

'As my mate, you can control my change on the non-full moons. I can become my full animal with your direction. Change me into my animal,' Nate added.

'Your animal?' Cassie replied, hoping her question got across. She didn't even know what his animal was. He never told her.

Nate shook his head. *'My animal. My blue-eyed animal.'*

Cassie then remembered that Whitney had green eyes when she transformed. The tiger Cassie had been spending time with had blue eyes. She was certain of that. She looked up at Nate, and he nodded along with her thoughts.

'Did you hear that?' she asked.

'Kind of. And yes. That was me,' he added. *'Now if you could be so kind to get this over with, I can then get all three of us out of here.'*

'You can?' Cassie asked.

'Damn, woman, quit talking and change me.'

While Cassie wanted to complain and get more explanation about everything, he was right. At this moment, it was just Jack left at the house.

Cassie looked at Nate and thought about the large tiger he was at times. She pictured his nice soft fur and large silent paws. It made so much more sense now how he was the alpha, being one of the largest predators in nature. She would be kicking herself for not noticing earlier, but now she didn't have time for that. She had to get out; they all had to before the monsters returned. She needed her tiger for that.

Nate shifted in an instant to the large orange and black tiger she had already met. The chains binding him broke like paper. He jumped over to Cassie.

'Move back,' he told her.

Cassie moved to the back of the cell, and with one swipe, his large claws cut through the bars as if they were butter. She climbed out the hole before running over to her friend, not hesitating before she added a drop of blood to her friend's mouth and forcing her to drink the potion. Whitney came to quickly.

"What happened—" Whitney got out before Cassie put her hand over her mouth. Whitney sat up and stared at her, eyes bugging as her gaze jumped around the room.

Tiger Nate stood still and looked at the door.

'We need to leave now. Climb on,' he ordered her.

Cassie hated taking orders and not thinking things through, but she understood the urgency of the situation. Nate was way better adapted for getting them out. She could always complain later.

"Go now," Cassie mouthed to her friend.

Whitney stood up, changing into her monster form in the process.

The barn door opened. Jared stood in the doorway. He stared in awe at the giant tiger that was racing toward him with Cassie on its back.

'Don't hurt him,' Cassie begged when Nate rammed into Jared. He kept his claws tucked in while he pushed Jared aside like a rag doll. Whitney kept in step right behind them as he cleared a path.

Cassie bent down close and held onto Nate's fur. He ran away from the house as quickly as Whitney had run to it. Wind whipped her hair around, and Cassie was forced to shut her eyes. She didn't need to see anyway. Anywhere her cousin wasn't was where she wanted to be. Tiger Nate came to an abrupt halt. Cassie took the cue that her ride was done. She didn't know how long they ran, but it seemed that he didn't stop going until they reached Cassie's home. She slid off his large, furry back. He transformed partially, back to the creature she had seen the night she was in the old cottage and Whitney was protecting her door.

'*Why?*' Cassie asked. She kind of preferred the large tiger instead.

'*We can't let anyone know we completed the binding. They planned to drain your magic at the binding. It won't work now because they won't have the strength to do it. That was the whole point before. They needed to use the magic of our binding to drain you. I'd prefer they don't know what's going on before we take over the clan,*' Nate explained.

'*Take over the clan?*' Cassie asked.

Half-tiger, half-monster Nate gave what Cassie thought maybe could pass as a smile.

'*When we're officially bonded, they have to make me alpha. There's no one to stop me.*' He gave a creepy sort of laugh in his monster form. Cassie wasn't in a laughing mood. In fact, she was exhausted, and still a little terrified that Jack would come back.

Nate gave his creepy laugh again.

'*He can't do that 'make you disappear' trick to you now. You're bonded. He's not strong enough to take two people at once, or he would have back at the school. Now if he tries to take you, he has to take me, too.*'

Nate seemed to have an answer for everything.

'*Go inside and get to bed. You look like you're going to pass out right here.*'

'*I can't just go inside. The coven knows where I live.*

They'll just come here to take me again,' Cassie complained. She was sick of running away, but she couldn't think of any other option.

'Oh, they won't be going in your house anytime soon,' Nate answered, motioning for her to move.

'How can you know that? You didn't even know that Owen and Nic were going to drug us before,' Cassie added.

'I promise you, no one is going to move up the binding now. You're safe. Trust me.'

Cassie looked at Nate. His limbs were longer than what seemed natural and bulked out at the major muscles. He was taller, but it wasn't like he was a tree trunk. His monster body was built more like a swimmer—wide shoulders and skinny waist. His lower half was covered in his normal tiger fur, and even his odd cat-like face looked tigerish. But it was his eyes. Physically, he looked very much like the other monster that had attacked her; the one whose red glowing eyes would haunt her dreams for months if not years, but not Nate. His glowing blue eyes told her that it was still him. Surprisingly, it had been him all along. Those blue eyes. He was her protector, and she could feel it even more strongly now.

Cassie walked up to her uncle's house and opened the door. She was safe with Nate outside protecting her. Cassie stopped in the doorway. Aunt Maria was asleep on the couch. She sat up immediately as Cassie crossed the threshold.

Maria ran to Cassie and pulled her into her arms.

"John! She came home," Maria yelled.

Maria held Cassie back at arm's length and looked her over, head to toe. John came barreling down the stairs. He was just as happy and surprised to see Cassie. He picked her up into a bear hug.

"How in earth did you get away from the coven?" John asked.

"The coven? Is that what they're called?" Cassie asked.

"They?" Maria asked.

"Yeah. My cousin Jack," Cassie replied, confused and just completely tired.

"Jack?" Maria's voice cracked. "They gave you to Jack?" Now there was anger behind her words. She looked at John and was ready to begin one of her wordy rants. Cassie knew she would only understand part of it when she stopped speaking English during the middle of it like normal.

"Can she deal with this in the morning?" Nate asked as he stepped into the room. "We kind of had a long day."

Maria's mouth dropped open. Then her rant was completely gone, and she began to laugh.

"Yes, yes, go to bed and explain it all in the morning," Maria said as John gave them both a strange look of confusion.

"I'm glad you're home," Cassie told Maria, hugging her.

Nate followed Cassie up to her room; she didn't need to turn around to know he was there. There was a weird feeling where she could almost say she was connected to Nate now with a string. She knew where he was at every instant, and even slightly could tell what sort of mood he was in. It was beyond strange.

"Get some sleep. I'm sure we will have to deal with everything tomorrow," Nate explained.

"And Whitney?"

"She's fine. She had the best excuse for everything. She was unconscious for all of it. It'll just be our story to tell." Nate pulled back the covers on her bed and patted the sheets.

"Has anyone ever told you that you're a bit bossy?" Cassie asked as she yawned and climbed into the covers. She had no energy left to argue with him.

"All the time. In fact, I remember this little girl when I was growing up who used to tell me that she was going to curse me if I kept bossing her around."

"She still might," Cassie replied as she laid her head on her pillow.

Every muscle in her body relaxed. She was beyond tired. *Why did he have to be right?*

"I'll be downstairs. You are safe here," Nate told her, touching her cheek gently. "I won't let anyone hurt my mate, ever."

"Hey, remember. Don't read any more into all of this. I had to add my blood to activate the spell," Cassie said with her eyes closed.

"Or you could have just lied and told him that since you never tried the potion on silver, it didn't work," Nate answered. Cassie hadn't thought of that. "Goodnight, my love."

The light in the room switched off. Cassie was finally alone. She cuddled into her covers. She was warm and safe. Her life was completely different, and it had all changed in just one week's time. All she wanted to do was join the coven and become a witch. Now she wasn't so sure. Everything was different. It seemed as though the answers to every secret were hidden behind lies. Her life went from boring to complicated with one fateful decision. It wasn't exactly what she expected, but it was her life and hers to figure out. Cassie couldn't keep any more coherent thoughts going. She was too drained. Her new life was exhausting— and kind of fun. But she was never going to admit that to Nate. Maybe she didn't know what moving up to a witchling apprentice meant, but she wouldn't change it for the world. She felt it in every fiber of her being. This was where she was meant to be, and everything that came with it was just one more adventure.

ACKNOWLEDGEMENTS

To you, the reader. Thank you for taking the time to read this story and go on the journey with me. If you liked it, please leave a review on your favorite online bookseller (or all of them!) and connect with me social media. The greatest help you can do to keep a writer going is to support them by spreading the word about their books.

Also I would like to thank my editors and cover designers. A good editor is essential to getting the story correct (and in my case- two editors). Thank you so much, Kathie at Kat's Eye Editing and Melissa at There for You Editing. It would not be the same book without them. Also a thanks to my proofer Ashton Brammer for going over the novel with a fine tooth comb to catch little errors that bug people. A thank-you to my *AMAZING* cover artist Jessica for such a pretty cover. An awesome cover helps get people interested. I greatly appreciate all those that can do what I cannot, like editors and cover designers. I'm thankful I was able to find wonderful professionals to work with on this book.

I'd also like to thank my hubby for continuing to push me further down the writing road. He gives me time when I need it to work on my stories. He encourages me to keep going each and every day on this adventure. And he does all the behind-the-scenes effort to make this work (have you seen my trailers- he is awesome!). This would be so much harder without his help. So thank you, B. for pushing me off the deep end (or the cliff as I see it sometimes). And a great big thanks to my little munchkins who keep me going from before the sun comes up 'til long after it sets. Love you AK, KB, and EM.

Thank you so much for taking the time to read my novel!!

 ABOUT B KRISTIN McMICHAEL

Originally from Wisconsin, B. Kristin currently resides in Ohio with her husband, three small children, and three cats. A former cell biologist, she now does the mom thing of chasing kids, baking cookies, and playing outside while writing full time. She is a fan of all YA/NA fantasy and science fiction. Find her at www.bkristinmcmichael.com and Twitter, Facebook, Instagram, and Goodreads under B. Kristin McMichael.

OTHER BOOKS BY
B KRISTIN McMICHAEL

- To Stand Beside Her

Chalcedony Chronicles
- Carnelian
- Chrysoprase
- Aventurine
- Chrysocolla

The Night Human World series:

The Blue Eyes Trilogy (series 1)
- The Legend of the Blue Eyes
- Becoming a Legend
- Winning the Legend

The Day Human Trilogy (series 2)
- The Day Human Prince
- The Day Human King
- The Day Human Way

The Skinwalkers Witchling Trilogy (series 3)
- The Witchling's Apprentice
- The Wendigo Witchling (2016)

www.ingramcontent.com/pod-product-compliance
Lightning Source LLC
Chambersburg PA
CBHW060931180626
46817CB00004B/1491